**Wanted: Housekeeper—
to care for four young,
lovable boys.**

Must be calm in any and all situations,
from story time to scraped knees.
No prior experience necessary,
but a love of children is a must.
A sharp eye and a good ear
would come in real handy.
If interested, and qualified,
please contact Bryan Marlowe.

D1040600

FAMILY

Marie FERRARELLA

Mother for Hire

First-Time
FATHERS

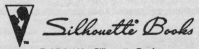

Silhouette Books

Published by Silhouette Books
America's Publisher of Contemporary Romance

SILHOUETTE BOOKS
300 East 42nd St.,
New York, N. Y. 10017

ISBN 0-373-82156-5

MOTHER FOR HIRE

Copyright © 1989 by Marie Rydzynski-Ferrarella

Dear Reader,

I have no idea where I'd be without my family. Possibly a lot saner, but I guarantee you, a lot lonelier. I am a family creature, a nester by trade. I mothered my younger brothers (which they took as being ordered around, but what did they know?) and once I was married, I would cut photos of babies out of magazines and put them into my husband's lunch bag, subtly hinting at what I wanted for Christmas— and always. For the sake of peace—and to keep from biting into a picture of a drooling baby—Charlie finally gave in. He figured I outnumbered him in sheer determination alone. But he's glad now I didn't give up. They make wonderful tax deductions. And they're great to hug.

In *Mother for Hire* I have a slightly different mix. The family there is made up of four boys and a dad. Three of them are carbon copies of each other and all four are full of the kind of energy needed to send a rocket to the moon. This is the kind of family Kate walked into. And the kind of family she wound up making her own. I think everyone got a pretty good deal. I hope you'll agree.

I wish you love and the very best of everything.

Marie Ferrarella

Please address questions and book requests to:
Silhouette Reader Service
U.S.: 3010 Walden Ave., P.O. Box 1325, Buffalo, NY 14269
Canadian: P.O. Box 609, Fort Erie, Ont. L2A 5X3

This book is dedicated to
St. Jude, Larry Thompson, my mother,
and everyone else
who was pulling for it.

Chapter One

He loved them.

He really loved them. But he was beginning to believe that they would be the death of him. And soon.

It was a hard thing to come to terms with, but he had to admit, if only to himself, that he really had his back up against a wall. Bryan Marlowe, esteemed criminal attorney, never at a loss for a tactic in the courtroom, was in a quandary over what his next move should be. There were, of course, boarding schools to consider, but he really didn't want to go that route. He didn't want to send them away as if they were just so much annoying excess baggage. Their mother's death had been enough of an emotional upheaval for them without their having something like that to cope with.

Besides, he strongly suspected that with their present lack of social graces, the boys would be returned to him posthaste.

It would be, he thought with a smile, tantamount to throwing a human boomerang. Several human boomerangs, he corrected himself as he looked at the culprits he had summoned into his den five minutes before. They stood lined up before him, fresh-faced and eager, with an innocence that barely disguised the mischief that lay underneath.

His gaze swept over his sons. The look on his face was capable of creating confidence and hope in his clients, chagrin and frustration in his opponents. Yet his sons appeared unaffected. Somehow, he thought, they saw through his act. And though they didn't quite understand why, they knew that he couldn't truly be stern with them.

"Mrs. Woolsey quit." Bryan's voice was quiet, subdued. He waited for signs of guilt or remorse within the ranks. He waited in vain.

Mrs. Woolsey, a well-bred woman in her late fifties who had arrived with glowing references, had been his housekeeper. More specifically she had been his *last* housekeeper. The last of a very long line. The woman had left, bag and baggage, earlier this morning, not even acknowledging Bryan when he spoke to her. She was too busy talking to herself, bewailing the day she had ever set foot in the Marlowe house. All in all, it had been a rather sad thing to watch, but he had no time to dwell on her plight. His own was too consuming at the moment.

"We saw her go," Mike, the eldest and the self-appointed spokesman for the lot, answered in a conversational voice.

He had the face of an angel, Bryan thought. They

all did. But beneath those innocent faces were four excitable boys.

"That's it?" Bryan had expected a little more this time, even from them. "'We saw her go?'"

"She took her suitcases," Trent chimed in.

Bryan sighed. If he was looking for guilt, he wasn't going to find it here. He tried a different approach. He and his sons shared a mutual affection that ran very deep. There was no point in losing his temper.

"Boys, you're going to have to help me out here. We've—no, *you've*—" he furrowed his brows, and at least one of the boys shifted a little "—gone through three housekeepers in a year." He sat on the edge of his desk and looked at each of them individually. "I need someone to be here to take care of you when I'm at work."

"We can take care of ourselves," Mike answered. The others nodded vigorously in agreement.

He had always encouraged them to be independent and self-sufficient. But at times it got out of hand. Like now. "At five and six, that's hardly possible."

"Maybe Mom can come back?"

The look on Trevor's face was hopeful. It tore at Bryan and mingled with the guilt and pain he still felt whenever he thought of Jill's death. It had been two years. He'd have thought that the pain would have disappeared by now. It hadn't. Not his, not theirs.

"We've been all through that, Trevor." He tried to keep the tightness from his voice. "Mom's not coming back." He cleared his throat. "We need a housekeeper," he repeated a little more firmly, guiding the conversation away from the subject of their mother. "Now, I want your word that if and when I find some nice lady foolhardy enough to take on this colossal job, you won't scare her off like you did the others." Though he felt a good deal older than his thirty-two years at the moment because of the morning's events, there was still a note of affection in his voice. Since Jill had died, he and the boys had drawn closer.

"But we didn't try to scare her, Dad," Mike insisted.

Bryan had to laugh. He pulled the boy to him and hugged him. Not to be outdone, his brothers pushed forward, each attempting to get a piece of their father. As they pushed and shoved in different directions, Bryan's legs were pulled out from under him. They all fell to the floor, a heap of swinging arms and legs. He was surrounded with squeals.

"Let's do it again, Dad!" begged Trent.

Bryan struggled back to his feet. "Maybe later." He brushed himself off. Perpetually sticky fingers attempted to aid him. Bryan sighed. "About your behavior with the housekeepers. Could you try to be a little less..." He searched for a word. "Energetic next time?"

"Sure, Dad," the boys chimed in.

He knew better. "Famous last words. Okay, council meeting's over. You can go."

"Will you still take me to the party?" Mike asked hopefully.

Bryan looked over his shoulder at the brief spread out on his desk. He had meant to get to it this morning. The case was Monday. Maybe later. "Sure, I'll take you. The rest of you will stay with your grandmother until I can pick you up. Try to remember that we want to keep Grandma in the family a few more years, okay?''

"Sure thing, Dad," one of them promised.

The boys piled out, running and making what someone who had obviously never had any children had once called a joyful noise. Bryan watched them go and ran a hand through his dark hair. He shook his head, wishing he had some sort of a permanent solution to the problem.

Bryan had had every intention of dropping Mike off, exchanging a few polite words with Jeremy, who was his associate, and his wife Alexis and then leaving. Since Bryan's mother had nobly offered to take the rest of the boys for the afternoon, that left him time to tackle the work he had brought home with him. Alexis's pleas for him to join the group of milling parents had fallen upon deaf ears. But on his way to the door, he glanced into the living room and noticed a young woman setting up equipment for a show of sorts. For an instant, the brief and his case were forgotten.

Glancing at Alexis, Bryan could see that she smugly took his hesitation to be a coup on her part. Bryan let his hostess go on thinking that as he eased himself over to the side for a better view.

There was something about the young woman Alexis had hired that caught his eye. For a moment, he was at a loss as to exactly what it was. He watched one of the children approach her. She flashed a grin in response, and then he had it. She was, he realized, instantly likable. Not dynamic, not sophisticated and polished. Likable. The difference between champagne and cool mountain water. Champagne could go flat. That didn't happen with mountain water.

The young woman was in the middle of setting up her props. Eager hands all around were trying to help her and consequently impeded her progress. It didn't seem to faze her, he noted. When one small guest sat on her guitar, she laughingly directed him to another seat, then took the instrument and spoke to it, asking it how it felt. The guitar answered, much to the awe and glee of her young audience.

And then she sang. A soft, haunting voice with just the lightest touch of an Irish lilt. Slowly the cacophony dissipated as, one by one, children and adults became mesmerized by her. Her voice filled his senses.

She was good, he thought. Very good.

Unconsciously Bryan accepted the glass of iced tea that Alexis pressed into his hands. He stood off to the side, and, leaning his shoulder against the wall, while he sipped his tea without tasting it, he watched the animated young woman in the midst of the ring of children.

"Who is she?" he asked Alexis in a low voice. Alexis beamed at his question. The party was an unqualified success even at this early stage.

"Isn't she just wonderful?" Alexis answered his question with a rhetorical one. "Julia Peterson told me that she was such a hit at her Paula's party. Julia heard about her through her bridge club. The woman has references a mile long. Of course, I wouldn't have just *anybody* arranging my son's party, so I had her checked out, and—"

Bryan knew that if he didn't interrupt, he'd be

standing here all day, listening to Alexis hook up facts with little care for their compatibility or the sense they made. "She does this for a living?"

There was nothing that Alexis liked better than to impart knowledge. "She's a student, I hear. She has a little business arranging children's parties to put herself through school." Alexis clasped her hands in front of her, the picture of contentment. "The children just adore her."

"Yes," Bryan agreed, "they do, don't they?" He noted that his own son seemed to be unusually docile and attentive to the silver-blond woman who now had a sad-eyed hound-dog puppet perched on her lap. She and the dog were engaged in an animated conversation. Bryan inclined his head, not taking his eyes off the young woman. "What's her name?"

"Kate Llewellyn. She's—"

Just then someone drew his hostess's attention from him. Bryan took the opportunity to edge away from Alexis and closer to Kate.

Desperate times bred desperate measures, he told himself. Monday morning was breathing down his neck. He couldn't be spared at the moment, so staying home wasn't possible. He was due in court and had no one to leave his sons with. In a pinch, he knew he could call on his mother again, but he hated to do it. She was getting on in years and was not up to what her grandsons, quite unintentionally, could dish out. A couple of hours was one thing. A whole day, even with school sandwiched in between, was quite another. He needed someone with more stamina. Someone preferably younger than the last three candidates had been. Someone with enough energy to keep up with his sons. They weren't bad, after all, just a bit overwhelming.

All right, he amended mentally with a smile, a lot overwhelming.

The children were all seated around Kate. Bryan placed his unfinished drink on a nearby table and joined the circle. He worked his way behind his son and tapped Mike on the shoulder. Mike half turned, not wanting to miss any of the show.

Bryan bent forward. "So, what do you think of her?" he whispered.

"She's neat."

He could hear the smile in his son's voice. That was good enough for him. He was going to do it. Money was no object, not where his sons were concerned.

Kate was aware of the tall, dark-haired man with the aristocratic face watching her. She was used to being observed, but the eyes that generally did the watching were smaller and saw things differently than an adult. She assumed that the distinguished-looking man in the light gray suit was a parent sizing her up for some future child's party that he was planning. Good, she thought. Lord knew she could use the money.

She put her observations into Shawn's mouth, and the hound dog raised his head in Bryan's direction. "Now what do you think that fine-lookin' gentleman over there is doin', Katie, watching us so intently and all?"

Bryan caught himself smiling in response. The

hound dog had an endearing Irish accent. It was a cute touch, he thought.

"She means you, Dad," Mike said in a loud whisper.

"Yes." Bryan nodded at Kate. "I know."

She pretended to turn her head in Bryan's direction, as if his presence was a total surprise. She leaned toward the puppet. "I don't know, Shawn. Maybe he's just a big kid himself and he wants to join in."

Shawn's ears shook as she moved his head up and down. He addressed Bryan. "Is that the way of it, sir? Are you just a big kid at heart?"

The children all giggled as they turned toward Bryan and waited for his response.

Bryan admired the way she had neatly turned the tables on him. Served him right for staring, he thought. "Maybe just for today," he answered.

"Well, there's no shame in being a kid, now, is there?" Kate asked the children. She received a chorus of nos for her answer. She looked back at Bryan and thought that he had the saddest gray eyes she had ever seen. She wondered about the cause behind it. "There's a little bit of a kid in all of us."

"Speak for yourself, girl," the dog retorted. "As for myself, it's a bit of the pup that's in me."

"Sorry, Shawn, I forgot."

The dog's head turned to give her what could only be construed as a baleful look. "'Tis all right. You're only human."

Bryan reaffirmed his decision. She'd do, all right. She'd do just fine. Now the only thing that remained was convincing her.

As Kate led the enthusiastic group of children in

one song after another, Bryan bided his time, retrieving his tea and nursing it until all the ice had melted and it had grown warm in his hands. He'd be damned, but it sounded as if she and the puppet were both singing at the same time. Hope began to stir in his veins. His colleagues had once said that he could argue St. Peter down from his heavenly post. Surely he could convince one woman to give up dragging a puppet around from house to house and to take on a job that had a great many benefits attached to it.

And several deterrents, he reminded himself. Still, she got on better with children than anyone he had ever met. And if he knew Alexis, she had been very thorough in checking the young woman's references out. So that took that worry away. The look on Mike's face told him that the boy was halfway into his first case of puppy love. That could go a long way toward helping quell his exuberance.

Finally the performance was over. Kate rose, to the protest of her audience.

Alexis flew to her rescue. "Now, now, children, it's time for the cake!"

The group of children seemed to hesitate as one, looking from Kate to the patio, where a long table bearing the cake and ice cream was set up.

"Shawn and I will join you in a few minutes," Kate promised.

The group broke up and made a beeline for the richly decorated table, leaving Kate to gather her props in peace. Bryan went into action.

"That was quite a show," Bryan told her.

Cornflower-blue eyes looked up at him. There was

a smile in them as well as one on her lips. "Thank you."

For some reason, when confronted with her gaze, his mind went blank. So where's your golden tongue now Marlowe? he asked himself as he cast about for a lead-in.

"Can I get you something to drink? Your throat must be dry after all that singing." He looked down at the puppet that she held in one hand. "Both your throats."

She gave a soft, charming laugh that made him think of wind chimes shifting in a summer breeze. "At times I think of Shawn as a living creature myself." She laid the puppet on top of the guitar. "That's the danger of getting caught up in make-believe."

"I think we all need a little make-believe at times." He said it because he surmised it was what she believed. Once, he had believed in that himself. But back then his life had been steadier, and he'd been a good deal more optimistic than he was now.

"It's nice to hear a man admit that." Kate looked around and saw nothing available to quench the thirst she had worked up. "Some soda would be lovely, if it wouldn't be putting you out."

"C'mon." Bryan took her by the hand. For some reason, it seemed to be the thing to do. Besides, she appeared to be the answer to his prayers, and he didn't want to take a chance on her escaping before he had a chance to make his proposition. "I know that Alexis has some in the refrigerator."

He was a man who liked to take charge, Kate

thought, silently leaving her hand in his. She wondered if his wife would mind that.

He led the way to the kitchen. "Don't mind us, Agnes," he said to the stoic woman preparing something at the sink. Short and built like a pear, Agnes had manned the kitchen for as many years as he had known the Howells. "We're just in search of some soda for the lady."

He opened the large refrigerator. It was teeming with groceries.

"There's enough food there to feed a small army," Kate said in awe as she looked over his shoulder.

Her breath feathered against his cheek as he bent down. Something distant stirred within him that disturbed him. He pushed it aside. "That aptly describes what Alexis has out there on the patio."

After moving a few things around, he located the beverages. There were several six-packs to choose from. He reached for the first handy can. Turning, he held it up for Kate's inspection. "This one all right?"

She took it from him gratefully. "It'll do just fine." She pulled open the ring on the top, and a tiny spray met her finger. "Just like champagne," she said, taking a long sip, "only better."

He watched her and thought to himself that she was a pretty woman, in a subtle sort of way. It was her radiance that hit him first, before her features became clear. He wondered if there was a man in her life and how that would affect the situation. He hoped there wasn't. He didn't need any more complications. That she would actually turn him down after he made his proposal never crossed his mind. Negative thinking had never won a case. "There'd be some who'd dispute that."

She lowered the can from her lips. The mouth was a little too wide, he thought, but the infectious smile more than made up for it. "Are you a champagne drinker, Mr.—?"

"Marlowe. Bryan Marlowe. And yes, on occasion, I do have a little, if there's something to celebrate." And if you accept, there'll be something to celebrate.

He cleared his throat. She raised her eyes to his, and he felt as if he had her undivided attention, as if there were no other distractions around. It was a heady feeling. It also made him feel oddly unsteady.

At another time and place, he would have prepared his buildup more carefully. But he was pressed for time. There was the brief to see to, and he had already used up a good portion of the morning. Maybe the direct approach would be best after all. He put his glass on the kitchen table and motioned her to sit in a chair. When she did, he pulled over another one and straddled it, facing her. "Forgive me for being blunt, Ms. Llewellyn, but do you make much money at this?"

What was he getting at, she wondered. He obviously wasn't out to hire her to arrange a party for his son. Just what did he have in mind, then?

"Enough," she answered a little guardedly. He was a stranger. There was no point in letting him know how tight things really were for her. "And there are some things you cannot put a price on."

"You really seem to like children."

"There's no 'seem' about it, Mr. Marlowe. I truly do like children. They're all beautiful little people, so ready to love, so ready to give if you know how to treat them. Most haven't found out about the world's disappointments yet.''

He thought about the looks on his sons' faces when they asked about their mother. Pushing that thought away, he kept his eyes on her face, studying her. Clean, pure lines. The more he looked, the more he realized that he liked what he saw—for his sons, he added quickly, then wondered why he felt the need to qualify his judgment.

''How would you like to make a lot more money, Ms. Llewellyn?''

Out of the corner of his eye, he saw Agnes give him a frosty look as she went on working. It didn't stop him.

Kate's eyes narrowed slightly as she tried to assess Bryan. She thought of herself as a fair judge of character and wouldn't have believed that someone like Bryan would proposition her, especially not with a housekeeper listening in. Of course, she reminded herself, she wasn't infallible.

''And just what is it that you'd be havin' in mind, Mr. Marlowe?'' The accent that she had grown up hearing tended to creep into her voice when her emotions were aroused.

He saw the wary look enter her eyes and realized what his words must have sounded like to her. ''Nothing improper, I assure you. I need someone to watch my sons.''

''Like a baby-sitter?'' she asked, confused. He was going to a great deal of trouble if all he wanted was a baby-sitter.

''No, like a housekeeper, except that it would be

more like a little-boy keeper.'' No one listening to
him would have ever guessed that he could evoke any
emotion he sought from a jury, he thought. But this
was too close to his heart. He knew this was why a
surgeon never operated on his own family. He'd make
a mess of it. He wasn't doing very well himself at the
moment. Still, the young woman before him wasn't
shaking her head and running off. There was still a
chance she'd agree. ''And I need her *now*.''

''That's a new one,'' Agnes mumbled audibly.

Kate laughed, and the momentary tension broke.
Bryan flashed her an almost sheepish grin. The man,
she thought, had a beautiful smile. ''What's your
hurry?''

''My housekeeper quit this morning.''

''Small wonder,'' Agnes piped up.

He threw the woman a disgruntled look. This was
going to be difficult enough without someone giving
a running commentary on the sidelines. Agnes was
familiar with his family situation, but that didn't give
her the right to be a hindrance.

Bryan gave Kate his sincerest look, one that came
from the bottom of his rather desperate soul. He was
tired of interviewing housekeepers, tired of seeing
them leave. This one would stay, he felt, if only he
could get her to agree. ''I really need someone to look
after my sons in the daytime.''

''You have more than one?''

Agnes laughed out loud, then turned up the water
pressure to drown herself out. Bryan thought it prudent to merely say, ''Yes.''

Kate rose. There was no point in leading the man
on. She didn't have the time for the kind of work he

had in mind. There were her studies to think of. "Well, you're a lucky man, Mr. Marlowe. Children are a blessing from God."

Agnes shut off the faucet and dried her hands. "More like a test."

Bryan opened his mouth to say something to Agnes, then thought that there was no point. The woman was right. He turned his attention back to Kate. There was an apologetic, but firm, look on her face. No one made this woman do what she didn't want to, he thought.

"I'm sorry, Mr. Marlowe, but I'm just not in the little-boy keeping business."

He put his hand on her shoulder. She felt frail to the touch. But he'd bet she had a will of iron. His sons needed a woman like this—kind, but firm. He tried one more time. "It wouldn't be much trouble."

She really wanted to help. He had a desperate look about him, for all his sophistication, and she had a weakness for wanting to make things right. But she also had an obligation to herself, and her family. The sooner she was out of school and in practice, the sooner she could send money home. There was more to think about here than just herself or a man with sad gray eyes. "Then I'm sure you won't have any difficulty filling the position."

He should have realized that it had been too good to be true. Prayers did not get answered, not his, and certainly not with such lightning speed. Still, he didn't want to give up. Something in his soul told him she was the right person. "If you decide to change your mind—" he dug into his breast pocket "—for any reason, here's my card." He wrote his address on the back. "I'll be home all weekend." He placed it into her upturned palm.

"Thank you for the soda. And the card." She held it up between her thumb and forefinger. "But I really have to be going now. The children are waiting."

And with that, the greatest hope in Bryan Marlowe's life walked out through the sliding-glass door, to be swallowed up by a sea of children.

Bryan looked over toward Agnes. The old woman lowered her gaze immediately and began fixing a tray of small crustless sandwiches. He moved toward her, picking up a sandwich from the tray. "How about you, Agnes?"

"Not on your life, Mr. Marlowe."

He took a bite. The sandwich tasted dry. "I didn't think so." He looked out onto the patio and sighed.

Chapter Two

It was past three o'clock when Kate finally managed to get away from the party. With Shawn safely tucked away in her purse and the guitar hidden within its battered case, Kate trudged toward the bus stop a mile and a half down the road. She thought wistfully of her little blue car, which was now residing within her mechanic's garage, led there by the whimsy of a capricious transmission and now held there by her inability to pay the repair bill until, perhaps, later on this month.

Kate caught the bus and headed for home.

Home for the last three years had been a tiny furnished apartment not too far away from the campus. At times like this, when she was separated from her car, she was grateful for that.

The sky was beginning to turn a shade of dull gray by the time Kate got off the bus an hour later. She walked quickly. The gloomy weather didn't dampen the bubbling intensity that coursed inside her. She always felt this way after performing for children. It was as if they charged her with their own energy. For days she lived on the enthusiasm they generated within her.

Stopping at the bank of mailboxes that stood just in front of her apartment, she fished out her key and opened the box with her name on it. There were only two letters inside. As she pulled them out, the smile on her face stiffened slightly. The top one was from the registrar's office. She opened it quickly.

It informed her that tuition fees were going up as of the next semester. Again.

"Lovely," she murmured. Shoving the letters into the pocket of her jacket, she took out her apartment key and picked up her guitar. Enthusiasm was quickly ebbing away.

Kate did a few mental calculations as she mechanically worked her key into the lock. She sighed. It was going to be tight, she thought. Very tight.

"A fine way to treat a poor working girl and her puppet," she murmured as she opened the door to her apartment. "Oh well, I guess it can be managed."

She searched her mind for a bright side and found none. The guitar case thudded to the worn carpet beside her shoulder bag. "Two meals instead of three." Kate pushed the door closed with her shoulder. "And maybe I can pick up another part-time job....

That would cut into her study time. At the moment, between the money her late uncle had left her, her savings from over the course of the years and the payment she received through the children's parties, she was just making ends meet. The letter from the registrar's office pulled those ends further apart.

Kate sank down on the couch, making plans. But those plans died with the second letter. It was from the management of the apartment complex where she lived. Never a good sign, she thought.

"This probably isn't going to tell me that they've decided to reduce the rents."

She didn't want to open it, but there was no point in sticking her head in the sand. That wasn't her way. Taking a deep breath, she tore off the edge of the envelope and read. The letter informed her that because of rising maintenance expenses, rents were going up as of the first of the month. She stared at the figure quoted on the Xeroxed page that had her name written in ink in the salutation. A line about the best-laid plans of mice and men flitted through her mind.

Kate leaned over the arm of the sofa, stretching to where she had dropped her purse. Pulling it over to her lap, she extracted Shawn. For a moment, she sat, stroking the puppet and thinking. Nothing came to mind. She looked down at the hangdog face.

"The way I see it, it's either go to school and sleep in the car—when I can ransom it—or have a place to live, get a regular nine-to-five job and forget all this foolishness about being a psychologist. It's taken me too long already, and a full-time job'll make it that much harder."

The expression on the puppet's face looked particularly morose. "No, you're right. I don't like either solution, either."

The word *foolishness* stuck out in her mind. Getting her degree wasn't foolishness. It had been her dream for a long time. And it was coming about slower than it should be. She glared ruefully at the letter from the registrar. At this rate, she'd be fifty before she could finally practice. She kicked off her shoes and drew her legs up onto the sofa, hugging her knees. The puppet, caught in her lap, rose up directly in front of her. There just had to be a way out.

She stared at the puppet, thinking. Soft gray eyes came to her mind. She remembered the card she had thoughtlessly stashed in her purse. Sliding the puppet off her lap, she began to rummage in earnest through her purse. Mr. Marlowe's card had worked its way down to the bottom.

Well, she thought, it would give her a place to live. She could forget about worrying about the rent. That would put her wages, whatever they might be, toward her tuition. But it wasn't going to be easy juggling school and taking care of a couple of young boys.

She stopped and realized that she didn't know exactly how many sons Bryan had. She had assumed it was two when he used the plural. But two or three, it shouldn't make that much of a difference. After all, hadn't she been the one who helped take care of ten siblings while she was growing up? She had still managed to get good grades in school and keep up with the endless chores that were part of life on a farm. This would be a little like reliving old times. After being part of such a large family, she missed the noise and commotion on occasion. She missed being part of a group.

And, she added, it would be wonderful on-the-job training.

She turned the card around in her hand thoughtfully. "At least," she decided aloud, looking at the address written there, "it's worth looking into."

Kate slipped her shoes back on. Threatening sky or not, she decided that she had better pay a visit to Mr. Bryan Marlowe right now if she was going to have any peace of mind tonight. Although she was basically the eternal optimist who believed that things would take care of themselves, money worries had a way of keeping her awake into the wee hours of the morning.

She reached for the bus schedule she kept on the coffee table, resigned to having to plot yet another intricate journey.

Bryan Marlowe lived in a house that bespoke his station in life and was a result not of birth but of hard work. His sons lacked for nothing, Bryan thought as he sat in the living room, trying to listen to them recite the events of the afternoon's stay at their grandmother's.

They lacked for nothing—except a competent housekeeper with the stamina of a drill sergeant and the disposition of Mother Teresa, Bryan amended. His thoughts turned to Kate with an impatience he was unaccustomed to. He had thought he had come upon the perfect solution when he had seen her at the party. Now he had to come up with another one.

He responded mechanically to the boys' occasional questions. They didn't seem to notice that his thoughts were elsewhere. They were too busy arguing. Bryan thumbed through the Yellow Pages on his lap, wondering if there was a section marked Saint.

Mike latched onto his sleeve and jerked hard. "Dad!"

From the look on the boy's face, Bryan realized that Mike had been trying to get his attention for a while. "What is it?"

Mike pointed to the large bay window directly behind him. "There's somebody coming up the block."

Since people were not an uncommon presence on their street, even when it was raining, Bryan wondered at his son's excited tone. He decided that it was just Mike's way of drawing his attention from the others. Bryan merely nodded without looking behind him. "Anyone we know?"

Now all the boys were clustered by the window. "Nope." The assessment came from one of them. Without looking directly at the speaker, Bryan was never certain which one was speaking. The triplets all tended to sound alike at this age.

He assumed it was a salesperson. "Then we don't want any."

"Yes we do, Dad," Mike cried. "It's *her*!"

The Yellow Pages slipped from Bryan's fingers. By *her*, Bryan guessed Mike could only mean the ventriloquist from the party. He had talked about nothing else since they had driven home. There was no other *her* in Mike's life that he knew of.

But walking up the block? Now? That was rather unusual in this weather. For the last hour, they had been experiencing a typical California downpour.

Bryan turned toward the window. It *was* her. She was coming up the front walk. There was a very determined look on her face. Bryan rose and quickly strode past his sons. He opened the door and was confronted with the sight of Kate standing before him, peering out from beneath her yellow hood, her silver-blond hair plastered against her face. The rest of her was encased in a bright yellow rain slicker. Despite that, she looked drenched.

Mike elbowed his father aside as he angled for a position in the doorway. "Hi!"

Kate smiled down at the boy. "Hello, Mike, how are you?"

Bryan was surprised that she remembered his name. There were, after all, some thirty children at the party. "Ms. Llewellyn, this is a very pleasant surprise."

She pushed her hood back from her head. Raindrops scattered down her face. Some were caught on her lashes. It made her eyes look brighter. Bryan told himself that he was letting his mind wander.

"You said you'd be in," she explained brightly.

Bryan decided the warmth he felt seeping into his body was because, from all appearances, his problem had suddenly been resolved. "Yes, I did. Won't you come in?"

She pushed her hair out of her eyes as she crossed the threshold. "I'd like that."

For a moment, he couldn't help staring.

"You're staring again, Mr. Marlowe." Was this a habit with him? "Is something wrong?" Had he changed his mind? Oh, please don't let him have changed his mind.

"Forgive me for asking, but why are you all wet?"

She laughed, relieved. "In case you haven't noticed—'' she ran her fingers through her hair ''—it's raining outside.''

''You don't own a car?''

''Only part-time. The rest of the time it lives with my mechanic. It's there right now, I'm afraid, waiting to be ransomed.''

He stared at her incredulously. ''You walked here?''

''From the bus stop. A little rain never hurt anything.'' She looked down. The rug around her feet was beginning to look damp. ''Except, perhaps, a rug.''

He waved away her comment, a rush of relief suddenly running through him. Maybe prayers did get answered once in a while. ''It won't be the first time. Come in.'' She was still standing in the foyer. ''Make yourself at home.'' He emphasized the last word.

Kate looked around as she entered the living room. It was a tastefully decorated house—everything she saw she associated with the rich. Good breeding was evident in the subdued elegance of the decor.

In a moment, she had something different to think about. She was surrounded by children. Identical children. Kate blinked. She thought she was seeing double. But as the images increased in number, she realized that it wasn't her vision that was responsible for what she was seeing. She was looking at three, no four, boys and if she counted Mike, who was just a tiny bit taller, all four seemed to be cut out of the same pattern.

She cast a sidelong glance at Bryan, who was watching her reaction intently.

"You wouldn't happen to work for Xerox, now would you?"

Bryan laughed. "No, I'm a lawyer."

She looked the boys over, still a little taken aback. The reason for Bryan's eagerness to hire her was rapidly becoming apparent.

"Can I take your raincoat?"

"Oh yes, thank you." She shrugged out of it, her eyes on the boys, who were very obviously assessing her as well.

As he stood behind her, Bryan let his eyes skim over her. She was lithe, with a figure that was more on the athletic side than voluptuous. That would help her, he imagined, when she was sprinting after the triplets.

On closer scrutiny, she didn't look all that much bigger than the charges he was intending to leave her with. Mrs. Woolsey had been close to six feet tall in her sensible shoes, and *she* hadn't been equal to his infamous legion of terror. Why did he feel that just because this young woman was armed with a sleepy-eyed, hangdog puppet, she was up to the task of taming his crew?

He didn't know why, but somehow he knew she was.

She turned to face him. Unintentionally his eyes lowered to her breasts, which were small and firm. His hands curled around the slicker. "Can I get you something to drink, to warm up?"

She laughed, the sound reminding him of wind chimes again. "You're always offering me something to drink. No, I'll pass, thank you kindly. I've come to discuss the position." She looked at the sunny faces looking up at her. "So we have Mike plus three." She glanced in his direction. "Are they—"

"Triplets," Bryan supplied.

"You're rarely blessed."

"That could be taken two ways," Bryan answered.

"I meant it in the best possible way." For a moment, she paused, uncertain as to how to proceed. Applying for a job of this sort was new to her.

"They're well behaved, Ms. Llewellyn. Aren't you, boys?"

Heads bobbed so enthusiastically, Kate had to fight to suppress a laugh.

"You'll hardly know they're here," Bryan said, lying through his teeth. It was the first time he could recall ever doing that. Just showed how truly desperate he was, he thought with no remorse.

Her eyes met his. He detected humor in them. Humor, intelligence and a good deal more, he suddenly thought, with premonition. Was he going to get more than he bargained for? Not if he was careful, he assured himself.

"I sincerely doubt that."

Bryan cleared his throat. "Well, um—"

She looked from one face to another. She would be able to tell them apart in time, she thought. There were subtle differences. One's hair was more tousled, another's smile was lopsided. She grinned at them, and all but one mirrored her expression—he looked more solemn than his brothers. "If they were always well behaved, they wouldn't be boys, now would they?"

The way she said it, Bryan dared to hope that she

didn't mind little boys, rowdy or otherwise, even if there were four of them.

"I guess not. But I'm hoping they'll grow out of it." Bryan hung her slicker on the antique coatrack by the door. He gestured her to an overstuffed chair, then perched on the arm of a sofa facing her. The boys surrounded her, four pairs of eyes unabashedly glued to this new woman in their lives.

She tousled the hair of the triplet nearest to her. "It will be soon enough, Mr. Marlowe. Soon enough, I'm afraid."

Not soon enough for me, Bryan thought wearily, then sprang into a small speech to clinch the deal. "The job—"

But she wasn't looking at him any longer. "What are your names?" she asked the triplets, having already met Mike.

Bryan folded his arms across his chest, intrigued that she ignored his words in order to acquaint herself with his sons.

A rush of names bombarded her.

"Trent."

"Travis."

"Trevor."

She looked back at Bryan. "Doesn't help with the confusion any, does it?"

He shrugged sheepishly, remembering searching through a name book right after the multiple birth. "It seemed a cute idea at the time."

"You could have thrown a girl in there." Kate laughed as Mike made a face. "It would have made things a mite easier."

Bryan shook his head slowly. "I don't do things

the easy way." He had never seen eyes twinkle before, had always thought the description rather absurd. But hers did.

"So I noticed."

"The job pays well, Ms. Llewellyn."

He quoted her a figure, and she looked at him in surprise. "Are you expecting me to take care of them, or adopt them?"

"Believe me," he said gravely, deciding to be honest. "You'll earn it."

She looked from one boy to another. Mischief, she thought. Sheer mischief. Well, her brothers, Kevin, Jon and Patrick had been like that, and she had handled them quite well. "You make it sound like a challenge."

You're blowing it, Bryan warned himself. "I didn't mean to." Truth won out. "But it will be."

She felt their eyes on her. It would have been hard to miss. Sizing me up, are you, boys? Well, you don't know the half of it. I'm a match for you, make no mistake about it. "I've never turned my back on a challenge."

He liked the determined, confident smile she gave him. "Then it's settled." He rose and extended his hand toward her, relief flooding his veins. When she hesitated taking it, he wondered if something was going to go wrong at the last moment.

She looked around. "Wouldn't Mrs. Marlowe want to interview me, as well?"

Bryan's expression sobered as he thought of Jill. "There is no Mrs. Marlowe."

Kate looked at the boys and then back at Bryan. "Had them by yourself, did you?" The serious expression did not fade. "That's humor, Mr. Marlowe," she said softly. "If you haven't a sense of it, I can't work here."

She began to rise, but he put his hand on her shoulder. Again, the thought of frailty struck him. Dressed in jeans and a soft cotton blouse that outlined her gentle curves, this young woman seemed very capable and strong. Frail was the last word that could be used to describe her.

"Ms. Llewellyn, I have four sons under the age of seven. If I didn't have a sense of humor, I wouldn't have been able to survive this long."

"You have a point." She wondered if Mrs. Marlowe had died suddenly. Was that why he didn't offer an explanation in front of the boys. "Well, do you have any questions for me?"

"When can you start?"

That wasn't what she meant. "As soon as you need me."

"Is now all right with you?"

For a lawyer, he certainly wasn't cautious, Kate thought. She could be an ax murderer for all he knew. Was he really that desperate? She glanced at the faces around her and thought of her brothers. Maybe he was, at that. "Don't you want to know anything about me?"

"You're breathing and you're willing, that's enough. Besides," he added, "Alexis Howell tells me that you have excellent references."

She gave him a ready smile. "That I do, Mr. Marlowe. Beginning with my mother."

No longer content to listen politely, Mike tugged at her arm. "Did you bring the dog?"

"Shawn?" She shook her head. "No, I'm afraid I left him at home."

"Will he be moving in, too?" The expression on Mike's face was hopeful.

"Absolutely."

Bryan thought it best if she wasn't completely overwhelmed by them the very first day. Placing himself between her and the boys as she rose, Bryan took her arm. "Would you like to see your room?"

Before she could nod, two of the boys cut Bryan off. They took possession of both of Kate's hands and ushered her off to the second floor, while the others shouted and led the way. Bryan followed, bringing up the rear. He should have known better, he thought. Oh well, she might as well find out exactly what she was up against.

They passed several rooms along the way. All were in a state of turmoil.

Kate turned to look at Bryan. "How long did you say it's been since your last housekeeper left?"

"She quit this morning."

"The boys work fast, Mr. Marlowe," she pronounced.

"You have a keen eye, Ms. Llewellyn."

The boys stopped leading her and opened the door directly in front of her. Kate stared at the white-and-blue room with its lacy curtains at the window. She walked in slowly.

This is a dream, right God? she thought, and I'll be waking up soon. I realize that. But please don't make it too soon.

"This is it?" she asked softly, surprise and wonder mingling in her voice.

He thought perhaps she was objecting to her accommodations. Bryan stepped forward, trying to find fault with the room. There wasn't any as far as he could see. "What's the matter, don't you like it?"

She turned to look at him. "Like it?" She laughed. "It's fantastic! My whole apartment could fit into it with room to spare."

Hope returned. "Then it's yes?"

She wanted to agree instantly, but there were her studies to think of. He had to understand what was important to her. Momentarily ignoring the four turned-up faces that surrounded her like blooming sunflowers, she looked only at Bryan. "I want you to understand that I'll be needing some time to study, Mr. Marlowe. I'm taking four courses at the university. Getting my degree is very important to me."

Was that all? "You'll have plenty of free time to study," he said with relief. At this point, he would have promised her anything to get her to agree to the position.

But she wasn't all that certain that he was listening. "You understand that the courses are during the day."

"What time?"

"Between nine and one."

"Perfect." His grin was warm, and it filtered through to her veins. She found herself reacting unconsciously and being surprised by it. "The boys are in school from eight until two. You can drop them off on your way to class and pick them up when you get back. What I really need is a baby-sitter for when they're home from school and I'm at work."

"We're not babies!" Mike protested.

"Young-men sitter," Kate amended with an eye on the boy. He settled down, as did the others.

"Until I get a housekeeper, though, I'd like you to prepare a light breakfast and dinner for the boys. All the major housework and everything else will be done by the housekeeper or a temporary cleaning woman until I can hire someone. I'm usually home by six or so. Evenings you'll be totally free to do your studying or whatever else you choose." He saw her mouth curve at his words. "All I need is for someone to take them to school and be here for them between two and six." Once again, he took her hand, as if that was enough to seal their bargain. "So what do you say, Kate? Is it a bargain?"

In the face of such persistence and given the nature of her own circumstances, there was nothing else to say. "With all these fine young men around me, what could I possibly say? It's a bargain."

"You won't regret this," Bryan assured her.

Mentally he crossed his fingers. There was no harm in having a positive attitude about this, he told himself. With a little bit of luck, Irish preferably, he wouldn't be far from wrong.

Chapter Three

Kate firmly believed in never putting off until tomorrow what she could do today. But Bryan gave new meaning to the old adage. Once the bargain had been struck between them, he had immediately offered to help her move in. No, *offered* was the wrong word, she decided as she heard his sharp knock on her door the next day. *Insisted* was more like it.

She opened the door, a greeting on her lips. It froze. It took her a moment to reconcile the man who stood on her doorstep with the man who had been surrounded by noisy children yesterday. He was dressed in jeans and a blue rugby shirt. Her initial impression of him, one of elegance, now had to be modified. He looked different, but good. Definitely good. The word that best suited the change was masculine. Before, he had been attractive in a sterile sort of way, a picture-perfect example of the successful lawyer. Now he looked real, earthy, yet still attractive.

Actually, more so.

She noted appreciatively that the shirt he wore molded itself against his muscular chest. The man was well rounded. Intelligence mixed with good looks and an excellent physique. A triple threat if ever there was one, she mused, absently wondering about the women who must be in his life.

"Hi." She looked around him. He was alone. "Where are the boys?"

"They're with my mother. I thought we'd get a lot more accomplished without their help."

She gestured him into the living room. "You know, I could've waited until the first of the month."

"Maybe you could have, but I couldn't." He looked around the small, square room and frowned slightly. The combination of beiges and browns that met his eye was drab and dull. It didn't match her personality, the little that he had glimpsed.

"My lease isn't up until the first," she emphasized as she carried a tray of iced coffee from the kitchen into the adjoining room. She set it on the coffee table. "Iced coffee. I hope you like it."

He took it as an invitation to sit, although he'd much rather get to work. Time was always precious to him. Bryan stretched out his long legs before him and took a tall glass into his hands. "Iced coffee is fine. And I'll reimburse you for the lease."

She sat down next to him. The sofa sagged in the center. She didn't seem to notice as her bare thigh brushed against his. He did. He noticed the white cut-offs, the graceful legs, everything. Considered an excellent judge of human nature, Bryan was somehow unable to pinpoint his own reaction to her.

"That's very kind of you." She paused, her eyes looking at him intently, almost studying him.

He wondered why, then decided that it was probably just her nature to be inquisitive. It was undoubtedly that trait that made her get along so well with children.

"Is there something you're not telling me about the job, Mr. Marlowe?"

The question took him by surprise, and for a second he couldn't respond. "Like what?"

Her cornflower-blue eyes met his over her glass. "Like you have a hundred-pound, man-eating canary in your den."

He laughed. It eased some of the tension he was unaccountably experiencing by sitting next to her. "I don't need a hundred-pound, man-eating canary in my den, I have the crew."

"The crew? Is that something like the plague?" she guessed, sipping her coffee and watching him over the rim of her glass.

She looked damned sexy, with her eyes raised like that. The thought both surprised and annoyed him. "In a way. The crew is what I call the boys."

She put her glass down on the coffee table and sighed softly with relief. She hadn't bitten off more than she could chew. "And that's all?"

"Kate, there is no 'all' when referring to the crew." He rolled the glass between his hands, unintentionally warming it. "I have to be honest. Since Jill—" He broke off abruptly and began again. "I've gone through five housekeepers in the last two years."

So that was her name. Jill. He piqued her curiosity.

There was pain when he said his wife's name. And then a curtain seemed to come down. Unconsciously she found herself envying Jill Marlowe. It must have been wonderful to have been loved so deeply.

She wondered how deep the hurt went and how raw. Something within her wanted to soothe it, to comfort him, but then she had always had a weakness for anyone in pain or trouble.

For now, you'll be leaving his hurt alone, she told herself sternly.

For now, perhaps, but not forever.

"I'm a lot sturdier than I look," she assured him, leaning forward. "The boys and I will get on fine." She rose and he followed suit. Kate felt as if she was putting him out. After all, he probably had a great many more important things to do than help her move. "You really didn't have to do this, Mr. Marlowe."

"Do what?"

"Help me move." She indicated the surrounding area. "I don't have that much to move, really. It's a furnished apartment." She took the two empty glasses back to the sink and rinsed them.

So she wasn't responsible for the dull furnishings. "Glad to hear that."

She stopped drying the glasses and looked at him a little oddly. "Excuse me?"

He grinned. She found that he looked like his sons when he did that, despite the difference in hair color. "What I meant was that this is a very dull room. I wouldn't have wanted to think that you picked out this furniture yourself."

"And why is that?"

Why indeed? Why did he care what colors appealed to her? That didn't figure into how competent she was at handling his rambunctious sons. "I'm not sure," he acknowledged with a half shrug. "It seemed to be the thing to say."

Now that made a hell of a lot of sense, he upbraided himself. Bryan usually hated things that made no sense. It had to be overwork, he decided.

Absently he noted the blue vase with fresh daisies on the low coffee table. A vivid testimony to life in an otherwise dreary room. Now that was her. He slid his thumb over a petal. Soft, silky. Yes, that was more like her. Touching the flower seemed to soothe him. Being soothed wasn't a condition he was much acquainted with in the past two years.

He realized that she was watching him curiously, a hint of amusement running along her generous mouth. He felt strangely awkward and searched for something to say. "All right, so the furniture isn't yours." He shifted restlessly. "What do you have to move?"

"Just books, clothes and a few kitchen utensils." She placed the glasses in a carton and closed it. "It wouldn't take me too long to bring them over."

He shoved his hands into his pockets. One eyebrow raised skeptically. "On the bus? You'd be in transit for a week. This'll be much simpler."

His thoughtfulness warmed her. It made her feel that she had, after all, made the right choice. She had never had any doubts about taking charge of the boys. It was Bryan who gave her pause. There was something there, something within his eyes that both appealed to her better instincts and warned her that she might be asking for trouble. "That's very nice of you."

She led the way into the bedroom. It was as small and crammed as the living room, dominated by a double bed with the most vivid bedspread he had ever seen: a patchwork quilt made up of velvet squares of kelly-green and gold.

Kate had disappeared into her closet. When she reappeared with an arm load of textbooks, she found him looking at the quilt.

"A present from the girls," she told him.

From the warmth in her voice, he knew that her ties to "the girls" went deep. "The girls?"

"My mother and sisters, and probably Kevin and Patrick and Jon, although they'd die before admitting it."

"Patrick, Kevin and Jon are—?"

"My brothers," she completed his sentence as she loaded the books into his arms.

"And they're the ones who have made you an expert on handling boys," he concluded.

"No, they're the ones who have made me an expert on mischief," she corrected. "I survived them, therefore I can survive anything."

He liked the confidence in her voice. "I certainly hope so." He looked down at the books in his arms. "Are all these yours?"

"Every last one. Read them from cover to worn cover, I have."

He glanced at the top book. "*The Headstrong Child.*" This certainly would come in handy, he reflected, once again congratulating himself on his choice. He looked up and saw the stack of photo albums on the shelf. "And the pictures? A hobby?"

"A family," she answered proudly.

He glanced down at her hand and felt an odd anticipation skimming through him that he couldn't put a name to. "You're not married, are you?" It didn't make sense, with her living like this, but stranger things had been true. This one point he wanted cleared up.

She laughed. "I haven't had time for that, although my mother certainly wishes I did and makes no bones about telling me so every chance she gets." She pulled down a few books herself and then nodded her head toward the door. Bryan began to walk and she followed him. "I miss them a lot—the family, I mean—but I had to move out here in order to go to school."

He held the door open for her with his back, and she passed him. The air felt brisk and clean. A good day for a new beginning, she thought enthusiastically. "It wasn't easy finding a good school, considering the money I had to spare for my education."

Bryan led the way to the navy-blue van he had parked outside her door. He had borrowed it just to help her move. "Lucky for me that you decided to settle here." He piled the books in the back, then leaned against the door as he watching her do the same.

Kate pushed the two stacks to the side, then looked up at him. "Oh now, don't go being too grateful."

"You're not going to change your mind, are you?"

She shook her head as she effortlessly slipped her arm through his and led him back to her apartment.

"No, but you are getting a pig in the poke, so to speak. You still don't know very much about me except that I'm a student, that putting words into a puppet's mouth comes easy for me, and that I can entertain children for a small space of time."

When she withdrew her arm, he found that he missed it. Silly, he thought. He followed her back into the bedroom. "I saw the look in your eyes as you were entertaining them. You enjoy it."

Balancing on a chair she had dragged into the walk-in closet for just this purpose, she reached toward the back of the shelf. Stretching, she managed to pull out books that had worked their way into the inner recesses of the shelf. "That I do." Her voice was muffled.

He was treated to the sight of her supple limbs as she balanced herself on the chair, reaching farther into the closet. He reminded himself that his only interest in her was as his sons' governess. He wasn't successful, not in the conviction nor in the effort of drawing his eyes away.

"And they enjoy you."

For such a petite person, she seemed to be all legs. No, that wasn't entirely true, he amended, thinking of her soft, firm breasts as they had appeared covered by a thin, wet blouse yesterday in his living room. He felt his body respond to his feelings and forced himself to steer his thoughts elsewhere.

Kate stepped off the chair, books in hand. He took them from her quickly, averting his eyes. He had a distinct feeling that she could read his thoughts. It was an absurd notion and he'd be the first to admit it, but it stuck with him, and he was taking no chances.

"I've been lucky," she told him.

"You've been good," he corrected. He waited until she took a load of her own before turning for the doorway. The puppet caught his eye. "Where'd you learn to do that?" He nodded at the puppet, which lay on the center of her bed.

"Shawn?" She put the books down on the bed and slipped the puppet on her hand. The dog's head moved in small circles, like someone working the kink out of his neck. "He evolved out of an old sock."

Bryan chuckled, leaning his hip against the wall and balancing the books before him. "Now that's thrifty. I just throw my old ones away."

Kate grinned, the memory of a fateful summer coming back to her. "I was eight and had broken my leg." Unconsciously her voice took on the lilt she had grown up with. "Oh, mad about it I was, lying there while the others were outside playing, enjoying the summer sun. So my Da—my father," she corrected herself when she saw the blank look on Bryan's face, "rode all the way into town that Saturday and got a book out of the library on ventriloquism. He had wanted to get one on magic, but they had only one and it was out. He handed the book to me and looked at me sternly."

She lowered her voice to approximate her father's, and Bryan could almost visualize the scene of a young, bedridden girl and her doting father.

"'Katherine Colleen,' he said—he liked to use both my names, you see—'you've too good a mind to be lying here, sulking and feeling sorry for yourself. This book'll show you how to entertain yourself.'"

She looked down at the puppet on her hand, and Bryan saw the fondness there.

With her free hand, Kate stroked the puppet's head. "He would've bought me a puppet, too, but we were too poor for that, what with all the mouths to feed and the doctor to pay for my leg." Her voice swelled as the memory faded back into the regions of her mind. She lifted her head proudly and looked at Bryan. "So I made a puppet out of an old sock and some yarn. And Shawn the First was born." She raised her puppet-covered hand. "This is Shawn the Third."

"What happened to Shawn the Second?"

"The poor darling wore out, doing shows." She took a deep breath, realizing that she was straying. She shook the puppet loose from her hand, letting it fall onto the bed, and picked up the books again. "Well, you didn't come here to hear me prattle on." She headed out the door.

"You're not prattling," he said, following her. "You're being entertaining."

She put the stack next to the other two on the floor of his van. "It's an occupational hazard, I'm afraid. My mother swears I was born talking."

He could believe it. He also found himself liking it. The women he interacted with on a regular basis were more sophisticated. There was a touch of remoteness, of unreality about them, as if they mentally censored their own words before they were uttered in order not to give away any more information than they felt would be flattering. Not that he cared, he told himself vehemently. Caring was something that he reserved only for his sons.

Still, he argued, there was no reason why he shouldn't find out a few pertinent things about the woman whom he was leaving in charge of the only people who mattered in his life. "Where is home?"

Kate looked over her shoulder as she reentered her apartment. "Originally?"

"Yes."

She stood up on the chair again and took down the last stack of books. She turned and handed them down to Bryan. "For my parents, a little town in Ireland." She stepped down, several albums of various colors clasped against her chest. "I was born just after they came to America and settled in a small town north of Oakland. My father had an older brother there to help him get started."

They made their way to the van with the last load. Bryan deposited her textbooks and reached for the albums. "At what?"

Rather than surrender them, she placed the albums gently beside the books. Her hand skimmed lovingly over the cover of the top collection before she looked back up at Bryan. "Farming." She lifted her head proudly. "I'm a farm girl."

He laughed. "That might come in handy when you're trying to round up my sons."

She caught his drift. "I'll have no trouble, Mr. Marlowe. They're just high-spirited."

He crossed his arms before him and leaned against the side of the van. "I'd like to hear you say that in about a week."

She gave a sharp nod, coupled with a confident smile. "All right, Mr. Marlowe, I will."

He wanted to tell her to call him Bryan, but knew that it wouldn't be quite the proper thing to do. Still, he didn't feel comfortable having her be so formal with him.

She is the nanny, the governess, he reminded himself, an employee. Not a friend.

But she could be, a voice within him whispered. He stifled it. He didn't need friends, he didn't need involvements. That way lay only trouble. And pain.

He glanced at the large stacks in the car. "You certainly have acquired a lot of textbooks."

"I believe in being thorough."

He could relate to that, he thought.

"And I like the subject." Kate began to walk into the apartment again. There were only a few personal effects left, besides the puppet and the bedspread.

He closed the door behind him. "What makes a farm girl want to be a child psychologist?"

"Come help with the bedspread," she called from the bedroom.

She came by giving orders easily, he thought, intrigued as he walked into the room to comply. He took the ends of the bedspread closest to him and folded the velvety item in half.

"Childhood should be a happy time." Between them the bedspread was folded in half again. "It's a sin when it's not. I believe each child has an inalienable right to be happy." She moved toward him with the corners of the bedspread, meeting his hands as she folded it again for the final time.

They were toe-to-toe, the bedspread a buffer between them. He looked down into her eyes. "That goes for adults, as well?"

Oh Lord, maybe you're not going to be that safe after all, Katie my girl, she thought as a sudden jolt passed through her, alerting her that something was there between them, and it wasn't just the velvet quilt. "Every adult was once a child. The right foundations—" She let her voice trail off significantly. She couldn't seem to concentrate on the topic, given the thoughts that were whipping through her active mind.

You have no other options open, Kate, and the man is desperate. You gave your word.

She always could argue herself into what she truly wanted to do, she reflected. Gently she slipped the bedspread from his hands and held it against her.

The moment hadn't gone unnoticed by Bryan, but he saw no reason to say so. "I see your point. I think I'm going to like you, Ms. Llewellyn," he said almost formally.

Then why aren't you smiling when you say that, she wondered. "Kate," she corrected. "That's good, because I feel I already like you." She nodded toward the suitcase in the closet. She had packed it earlier that morning. "If you take that, we'll almost be done."

He picked it up and found that it was heavier than it looked. "You always assess everyone so quickly?"

"Yes. And I find that I'm usually right." She turned and looked around the room, then walked into the living room. "Except for that box there—" she nodded at the box on the kitchen table "—we're finished."

She turned back to Bryan and gave him a smile

that he was finding to be more and more infectious. She was catching, he realized. She was a happy soul, and being around her made him feel less inclined to dwell on all that was wrong with his life. She was going to be a good influence on his sons, he decided.

That is, if she lasted. Despite her words to the contrary, he knew the reality of it. His sons were too high-spirited for the last four housekeepers and the one before that had conveniently married. He wondered if it was fair to Kate, letting the triplets and Mike loose on her.

But he knew he didn't have a choice.

"Not much to show for twenty-six years, is it?" she said with half a laugh as she surveyed the things in the back of his van. The bedspread lay over the books and albums like a protective awning.

Bryan closed the doors and secured them. "I know people who have a lot less."

She liked his answer. "So do I, Mr. Marlowe. So do I." She walked in front of him to the passenger side. He caught a whiff of a subtle scent and couldn't decide whether it was perfume or a particular fragrance all her own. A sweetness seeped into him, bypassing all his best efforts to effectively block it.

On the way back to the house, they picked up his sons. She met Bryan's mother and found the resemblance to be uncanny. The weariness was also hard to miss.

"I hope you last, Kate," Alicia Marlowe said, shaking her hand after Bryan had made a quick introduction.

"I fully intend to," Kate assured her.

"The last lady we had lasted a month," one of the triplets informed her solemnly.

"Three weeks," Mike corrected him impatiently.

Another one of the boys tugged at the hem of her blouse. "How long are you going to last?"

"Longer," she answered briskly.

The lady has style, Bryan thought. He clapped his hands together. "Let's go, guys." Bryan herded the quartet in front of him. "Your grandmother looks like she needs her rest."

"Nothing a couple of vitamin B-twelve shots and a week's worth of sleep couldn't cure," Alicia said. She took Kate's hand again in both of hers. "I wish you luck, dear. I know you'll need it."

There was only time to say goodbye before Kate had to hurry to catch up. She climbed back into the seat in the front while the boys fought over who was going to sit where in the back. Kate made mental notes, studying the situation.

Bryan slid into the seat next to hers and gave her a look that said, "See?" He started up the van. The noise of the engine was drowned out by the raised voices in the back.

Mike leaned forward and laced his hands on the back of Kate's seat. "Gee, we're glad you're here. Now we're gonna have fun!"

Kate twisted around in her seat until she could look at the boy. She raised her eyebrows, and they slipped beneath her wispy bangs. There was a warm smile on her lips, but her voice was firm. "If you're thinking that we're going to be having nothing but candy for dinner and cartoons for breakfast, young man, I'm afraid that you're sadly mistaken."

Mike's face fell. He looked as if he had been betrayed. "But I thought you'd play with us," Mike whined.

She turned in the bucket seat and leaned over so that she could raise his chin with her hand. She looked into the blue eyes and saw so much there. "That I will. But I'm going to work with you, too—and teach you to like it."

Bryan made a sharp left. Kate tilted in her seat. "If you pull that off, Kate, you're one rare lady indeed."

She settled back into her seat. "Miracles are my specialty, Mr. Marlowe," she told him with a toss of her head.

He wasn't quite certain if she was kidding or not. He had a feeling that she wasn't. More power to you, Katherine Colleen Llewellyn, he thought. But the odds aren't in your favor. He thought it prudent not to mention that fact aloud any more than he already had.

When they reached the house, the four in the back jumped out, pushing for the right to be first as they all ran for the front door.

"Boys!" Kate called out.

Collectively they turned and looked at her, waiting.

"I need your help."

"Help?" Travis echoed.

"Yes." She crooked her finger and beckoned them back.

Uncertainly the boys walked back to the rear of the van. She gestured to the van's opened doors and the books that lay all over the floor. "There're a lot of books here, and your father can't be expected to carry them all himself now, can he? Not when he's got four such strong, handsome sons to help him.''

Bryan inclined his head as he whispered, ''Which side of the Blarney stone did you say you were born on?''

''The right side.'' She counted out three books at a time and deposited them into the outstretched hands. She nodded her head approvingly. The smile she wore was for each boy individually. ''Now, no pushing boys, there's plenty here for everybody, I promise you.'' She turned toward a bemused-looking Bryan. ''Mr. Marlowe, if you'd be so kind as to open the front door for the boys and me, we'll be getting on with this.''

And get on with it she did, much to Bryan's surprise. He hadn't expected to see anything like this so soon. Actually, he hadn't expected to see anything like this at all.

Damn, you're good, lady, he thought in growing admiration.

Leading the pack and carrying an arm load of books herself, Kate walked into the house and up the stairs to what was now her room.

''Just anywhere'll do, boys. I haven't decided where to put them yet.''

On the fourth trip from the van, one of the triplets wearily waved his hand at all the books that had been lugged into the room. ''Are you really this smart, Katie?'' The others stared at her questioningly.

''No,'' she confessed, ''but I plan to be.''

''I'd say you had a very good head start,'' Bryan told her as he came up the rear. ''I've never seen them this eager to do work.''

"All it takes is appealing to the finer nature. Everyone has one." A smile played with her lips. "Some just hide it a bit better than others." She slipped by him in the doorway. "If you'll excuse me, I have to supervise the next shift."

As she edged past him, their bodies brushed against each other for one moment. Kate raised her eyes up, and they looked at each other. Bryan felt touched by sunshine and stood where he was for a split second before he backed up. "Sorry," he murmured.

"Nothing to be sorry about," she answered softly as he walked away.

"I'm not so sure about that," Bryan said under his breath.

Instead of following her, he stood where he was, frozen in thought. Something had happened just then, something he would have usually called just a normal male reaction to a woman, except that it didn't exactly feel that way.

That's because you've kept yourself away from women for so long, he told himself. See what prolonged celibacy will do?

The celibacy was by choice. He found that his family and his practice filled his hours adequately enough. And if he was otherwise occupied, he couldn't make mistakes. It was because of his own mistake that Jill had died. He couldn't afford anything else like that on his conscience.

"Did you say my duties will include making dinner for the family?" Kate asked as she returned to the room with her suitcase.

He came to life and took it from her. "Until I can

hire a housekeeper to take care of those details, I thought that mostly we'd eat out—"

She let him get no further. "Eat out, indeed. Do you know what they put in food these days?"

He was going to hazard a guess, but never got the opportunity.

"If you'll show me the way to the kitchen, I can get on with it."

That seemed to be her favorite phrase, he thought. He wondered if the woman would ever let him finish a statement. "By all means," he acknowledged, leading the way down the stairs, "let's get on with it."

Chapter Four

Kate hadn't bothered turning on the light in her room when she walked in. Bright moonlight streamed in through the large window adjacent to her bed, high-lighting the room, softening the corners, giving it an ethereal quality. She sat on the cushioned window seat, her legs curled under her. The window looked out onto the backyard, a good deal of which was hidden in shadows. But from what she could see, a huge swing set dominated the left side of the grounds. Near it was a sandbox and a pool. It was a backyard made for children.

It was a good sign, she thought.

The soft, dreamy effect created by the moonlight was partially negated by the high-pitched, animated discussion drifting in through the south wall. Her room was next to the one occupied by the triplets. From the sound of it, two of them were arguing.

Kate pulled her knees to her chest and clasped her

hands around them for support. She knew she should take one last look at her Psych 12 notes before going to bed tonight. She had a test tomorrow. But she couldn't work up the energy. It had been a long day. An eventful day. Perhaps, she mused, wiggling her bare toes, even a turning point in her life. She had a funny feeling about all this. And she was a great believer in destiny. Things that were meant to happen *did* happen.

She exhaled a soft, contented sigh. She was going to like it here—noise, she thought looking at the south wall, notwithstanding.

A short, hesitant rap on the door caught her attention. She raised her head and looked toward the door, which she realized was slightly ajar. The hall light outlined its perimeter.

"Yes?" she called out.

She wondered if it was Bryan with last-minute instructions. He seemed the type who liked order. She swung her legs down, but remained seated, her hands balanced on the sill on either side of her.

Kate's "yes" was obviously interpreted as an invitation by the person on the other side of her bedroom door. Slowly the door opened. One of the triplets stood there, a large book firmly grasped in his hand. He squinted.

"Katie?" The voice was filled with uncertainty. He made no move to enter the dark room.

"Here."

Kate sensed more than saw his uneasiness. She rose and crossed to him.

He stayed where he was, bathed in the hall light.

As long as he had light, he was all right. It seemed to be his security blanket.

Curiosity got the better of him. ''What are you doing in the dark?''

''Being happy,'' she answered simply. She placed her hand on his shoulder. He jumped, slightly rigid. This one wasn't too certain about her, she thought. He was going to take more work than the others.

''In the dark?'' Astonishment echoed in his words.

''Happiness doesn't hinge upon light, Trevor.'' She reached out and flipped the switch on the wall next to the boy. The threatening shadows dissolved into nothingness as light claimed the room.

Only then did the boy look certain enough to venture into the room. Two steps in and he stopped, suddenly hit by a realization. ''How come you know which one I am?''

''Why shouldn't I?''

He shrugged. ''The other ladies Daddy brought here couldn't tell us apart. 'Specially the last one. She couldn't even tell which one was Mike.'' Trevor cocked his head to the side like an inquisitive little bird. ''How come you can?''

''Well,'' she began thoughtfully as she ushered him toward her bed, ''you introduced yourself to me. I never forget a face,'' she told him solemnly. Kate sat down and patted the spot next to her.

Trevor struggled to climb up. She noticed that he seemed extraordinarily careful not to wrinkle her comforter. A thoughtful whirlwind, she mused with a smile. But then, she had already identified him as the sensitive one in the group.

Trevor righted himself next to Kate on the bed as

best he could, his short, jeans-clad legs sticking out straight in front of him. "But my face is like the others," he protested.

"No, it's not." She touched his nose affectionately. He drew back a little, and she pretended not to notice. Lots of work, she amended silently. "Your smile is a little different from your brothers'. And your eyes are more serious."

"Is that bad?"

Why did he look at things so negatively, she wondered. He was awfully young for that. "No, that's just you." She smiled at him warmly. "Special."

He thought this one over. "Special?"

"Sure, everyone is special in his own way, even if he's one of a set of triplets." She could see that he was going to chew on that one for a while, but it did please him. Kate eyed the book he had kept clutched in his hand as he had climbed up on her bed. "What do you have there?"

He looked down at the brightly decorated cover before he answered. "A book. I thought maybe you could read this—to the other guys, I mean," he added quickly. "I don't really like fairy tales much." Shyness crept into his voice. Trevor was the youngest of the triplets, by a minute and a half, his brothers had informed her at dinner. He also appeared to be the most insecure one, Kate thought. He reminded her of her brother Kevin.

Trevor drew a deep breath and then blurted out, "That's what mommies on TV do."

Oh-oh. She had to remedy this one fast. She didn't want him getting things tangled up in his head. Kate slipped her arm around his small shoulders. "I'm going to be your friend, Trevor, not your mommy."

But Trevor shook his head. "Yes, you are. You're a mommy for hire. I heard my daddy tell Grandma that's what he was looking for. And now he's found you."

Kate started to correct this misguided notion when Trevor pushed the book toward her. He didn't seem to want her to deny his pronouncement. "Read me something. First."

"You mean before I read this to all of you?" He was dying for attention, wasn't he? The little one, lost in the crowd. Yes, just like Kevin. Kate's heart went out to him.

Trevor's blond head bobbed up and down. "I think maybe I should try this book out—to see if it's good enough for them to hear." He looked up at her solemnly.

Kate smiled at the innocent ploy. "Seems like a good idea to me." She flipped open the book. "Which story did you have in mind?"

Trevor peered over her arm, then jabbed a small finger at a page. "That one looks okay."

Kate looked at the title. "Goldilocks and the Three Bears?"

"Is Goldilocks a girl?"

"'Fraid so."

Trevor frowned.

Ah, a budding chauvinist, she thought. More and more like Kevin used to be. We'll get that out of you, my lad. "But two of the bears are boys," Kate offered.

Trevor shrugged, obviously torn. "Okay, I guess."

"Very democratic of you, Trevor," Kate said, with a nod of her head. She tousled his hair.

The corners of Trevor's mouth rose a little in a small smile. He didn't quite understand her, but he responded to her tone. Then, to Kate's surprise and pleasure, Trevor snuggled up against her as she was reading. Not all at once, but gradually, his guard slowly dissolving. Kate wove her arm around his small shoulders and kept him against her as she held the book and read.

Kate remembered home and felt a bittersweet ache as memories of her reading to her brothers and sisters filtered through her mind. She continued reading, bringing an age-old tale to life for a boy who had never heard it before.

Always a first time, Kate thought fondly.

She used different voices for each character and was rewarded with soft giggles. When they stopped, she noticed that Trevor's eyes were drooping. She smiled to herself and continued reading.

Trevor lasted until the second-to-last paragraph. Kate closed the book slowly. The sound of even breathing filled the air. Gently she put him down on the comforter. He curled over to his side, never waking.

Kate brushed the hair from his face. "I guess this will do for the others, then."

There was a sharp knock on her door.

"My, but this is a busy house," she murmured to herself as she rose from the bed. But that was just the way she liked it. Silence had its place, but she was partial to it only in very small increments.

She opened the door all the way, expecting to see

another short visitor. She had to raise her eyes. Bryan stood in the doorway. He looked a little uncomfortable, she thought, as if he'd rather be somewhere else. She wondered why.

Bryan was supposed to be working on the brief that was still waiting for his attention. Instead, his steps had taken him past his den and brought him here, to her doorway. Telling himself that he was just being helpful in settling Kate in didn't quite ring true, even to his ear. But he refused to explore it any further. "Um, I just wanted to know if you have everything you need."

"More than everything," she answered.

"Excuse me?"

In reply to his puzzled look, Kate stepped back and let him see the sleeping boy on her bedspread. "He wanted me to read him a story. Said he was testing it out for his brothers."

Bryan looked even more puzzled. "Trevor?" He couldn't believe it.

She wondered at his obvious surprise. Or was he guessing at which of the boys it was? "That's the one. Do you have trouble telling them apart?"

"No, but Trevor's been rather withdrawn with all the other women I've hired." It didn't seem possible. Trevor was the one he worried about. Trevor was the one who seemed to mind Jill's passing the most. It seemed incredible that he should seek Kate out so soon. Though amazed, Bryan felt a sense of satisfaction at having hired Kate. Maybe things were finally going to flow on an even keel—at least for the boys.

"I did notice a little bit of hesitance on his part, but I thought it was because I was new."

Bryan crossed the room to the bed and looked down at the sleeping boy. "No, he's been that way since—" He stopped abruptly.

Kate came up behind him. Even though she couldn't see his face, she could feel a wall form. Like father, like son. Her work was really cut out for her, she thought.

Bryan scooped the sleeping child up into his arms, then turned to face her. His manner was composed again. His face gave away no hint of what he was thinking.

"I'm sorry about this, Kate."

"Nothing to be sorry about, Mr. Marlowe." She ran a hand through the ruffled blond hair that had wantonly fallen over Trevor's eyes again. "Little boys do fall asleep."

He felt an unaccountable pang, having her stand there like that, touching his son so lovingly. Somewhere deep down, he still wanted a woman to love who loved his family in return. He blocked out the momentary flight of fancy.

You'd think you would've learned your lesson.

"Not usually on their nanny's bed the first night she's here." He hesitated. It was such an archaic, unsuitable word. "Do you mind me calling you that?"

"What? Nanny?"

Bryan nodded.

Kate smiled and shook her head. "It has a nice, old-fashioned, comfortable ring to it. No, I don't mind."

The name might have an old-fashioned, comfortable ring to it, but there was nothing else about the woman before him to suggest that, Bryan couldn't help thinking. He didn't know why, but the word comfortable didn't fit in with a description of her. Though she was pleasant and warm, and easy to talk to, he just wasn't comfortable around her, and he didn't know why. Or maybe he did but couldn't admit it to himself.

Even now, with his son acting as a physical barrier, there was something unsettling in the air between them, something charged. It was almost tangible. Maybe it was because it had been so long since there had been a young woman in the house. Mrs. Woolsey and the housekeepers before her had seen their youths a generation ago. Several generations ago. Was it possible that he had made a mistake hiring someone so young after all?

No, look at the way Trevor had reacted. It wasn't a mistake. At least, not for his sons.

Silence hung between them. Bryan searched for something to say. For him, it was an alien feeling of awkwardness. He used pregnant silences deftly when questioning witnesses on the stand.

He cleared his throat. "Well, if you won't be needing anything—" he edged out the door "—then good night."

"Good night, Mr. Marlowe. Oh, he might miss this in the morning." She held up the book and then tucked it beneath Bryan's arm. She tugged to make sure the book was firmly in place, then patted his arm with a grin.

Obviously she's used to touching people, Bryan thought as he left the room. He, by nature, was not a toucher. Not anymore.

Her smile lingered on in his mind as he walked into his sons' room.

"All right, I've given you the name and address of their school. Are there any questions, Kate?"

Kate turned from the stove, a platter of pancakes in her hands. "Only one."

He knew this was too simple. "Yes?"

She placed the platter in front of his place setting and began to put pancakes on his plate. "Would you like syrup or honey on your pancakes?"

Bryan sighed trying to hide his annoyance. He was running late. "I meant of a more important nature."

His impatient tone didn't put her off. "Breakfast is important, Mr. Marlowe." Around them, the usually animated conversation had dissipated. The boys all watched in awe and glee as the new governess appeared to be disciplining their father.

Bryan took a quick gulp of coffee from his cup and put it down. "I don't have time for breakfast." That was to be the end of it.

One look at her face told him he had miscalculated. Who was in charge here, anyway?

With a gentle hand on his shoulder, Kate eased Bryan down in his seat, then pushed the loaded plate closer toward him. Four pairs of eyes watched in relative wonder. "It won't take more than five minutes to eat this, and it'll save you grabbing a doughnut at ten."

He stared at her. Just what did she think she was doing? "I don't eat doughnuts."

She set the syrup and butter dish in front of him,

audaciously. "Maybe not, but you do eat. I saw you eating last night."

The boys giggled.

Bryan gave them a silencing look then tried it on Kate. To no avail. "Of course I eat, but—"

"Without a good breakfast, people tend to be short-tempered," she said mildly as she placed pancakes on the boys' plates.

He worked to maintain patience. "I am not short-tempered, Ms. Llewellyn."

She gave him an infuriatingly knowing look over her shoulder before she went on with the division of pancakes. "Would you care to take a vote on that?"

He watched her as she poured the syrup on Trevor's serving. "Kate, I hired you for the boys."

Kate stopped to pour herself a cup of coffee. "I'm aware of that."

"The definition of a boy is someone below the age of thirty-two years."

Kate took a long sip and swallowed before she answered. "There's a boy inside of every man." Again Kate pushed the plate closer toward him.

"Ah, the philosophy your puppet taught you." He had meant it with a touch of sarcasm.

The touch failed. It brought, instead, a pleased smile. "You remembered." Her expression grew slightly more serious. "You know, you could have eaten half your breakfast already, Mr. Marlowe, in the time you've spent talking to me."

Tactfully she had used the word *talking* instead of the one she meant, *arguing*. He saw his sons grinning at him.

"I suppose I'm not getting out until I eat this," he

said grudgingly. But something inside of him liked the fact that someone cared if he had breakfast of not. It had been a very long time.

"You catch on fast, Mr. Marlowe."

He had breakfast for the first time in years.

Kate raised her eyebrows as Bryan rose from his seat. His plate was clean. "Well?"

He stopped. "What, is there something else you want me to eat?"

Kate stood up and started to pick up his empty plate. The boys were squabbling over who would get the last pancake. Without skipping a beat, Kate cut it in four and distributed the pieces. "No, but don't you feel better?"

He liked the way she handled the situation of the last pancake, but he was still annoyed that she included him in with her charges. "I feel full."

She nodded, satisfied. "I'll accept that as a yes."

She was incorrigible. Bryan muttered under his breath. Kate tactfully did not ask him to repeat himself. She took his plate over to the sink.

Bryan followed her. "Here." He placed something into her hand.

Kate looked down to see a key ring.

"This," he pointed to a large key, "is for the front door. This little one is for the garage. And this one…" he accidentally ran his finger along the palm of her hand. The same odd, warm feeling flittered through him as before. Damn, she was too attractive for her own good. For *his* own good. "This one," he repeated, trying to ignore the effect her raised eyes were having on him, "is for the blue Mercedes station wagon in the garage."

"The Mercedes?" she echoed. She looked down at the key and then raised her eyes to his again.

They were definitely too blue, he decided. Like the sky shining into his soul. He realized that she was quiet. "Why, Ms. Llewellyn, I do believe you're speechless." He chuckled. "I didn't think that was a possibility with you."

She turned the key over in her hand. "I've never driven anything except a little Mustang—if you don't count the tractor."

He tried to visualize her driving a tractor and failed. "I don't. And I don't see you taking my sons to school on the bus. You'll have full use of the Mercedes. That means you can use it to go to classes as well."

"Well," she considered, "just until my car is out of the shop." She slipped the keys into the front pocket of her jeans.

Bryan squelched a sudden, surprising urge to follow the path her hand had taken.

"Thank you." A soft, musing smile slid across her lips. "It must be nice to be well-off enough not to care if someone else is driving your Mercedes."

He turned and picked up his attaché case where he had left it next to his chair. "Pragmatic, at the moment."

"Are you always pragmatic?"

He checked to see that all his papers were inside the case. "Always."

Kate crossed back to the table. "I'm sorry."

He snapped the case closed. "Are you apologizing for probing?"

"No, I'm sorry that you're always pragmatic. You miss half the fun that way."

"Of what?"

"Life."

Now she sounded like Pollyanna. "Life isn't fun, Kate. It's just there, to be bested. And in the end, it bests us."

She glanced at the boys and wondered if they understood what he was saying. She sincerely hoped not. But her main source of concern at the moment was Bryan. His wounds must run deep for him to believe what he had just said. "Oh, Mr. Marlowe, I *am* sorry."

Her words, her sentiment, made him uncomfortable again. And when he was uncomfortable, he didn't feel in control, the way he normally did. What was there about this woman with cornflower-blue eyes that robbed him of his hard-won edge? Was it going to continue like this?

"Don't be sorry, just be efficient." He took something out of his wallet. "Here."

She looked at the charge card he handed her. "More gifts?"

"The boys are overdue for spring clothes. The last housekeeper refused to go to the store with them, and I haven't had the opportunity. If you don't mind, after you pick them up, take them to Robinson's and get them outfitted."

Out of the corner of her eye, she saw the boys abandoning the table in a rush. "Plates to the sink, boys." She pointed at the cluttered table.

"But Daddy didn't," Travis protested.

"And when you pay my salary, you won't have to, either. Sink." She pointed behind her.

Reluctantly the foursome picked up their plates and began to trudge to the sink.

"Don't forget the glasses and forks." Glasses clinked. "Gently boys, gently. Your Dad doesn't want to buy a new set of glasses."

"Not this week, anyway," Bryan added.

While the crew of four deposited their dirty dishes in the sink, Kate pocketed the plastic card. "No specifics?" she asked Bryan.

"Yes." He checked his watch. Late. Bryan hurried toward the front door with Kate right behind him, waiting for him to finish. "I'd rather the damages didn't come to more than five hundred dollars."

"For the clothes?"

"No, for the breakage."

"I don't understand."

He pulled open the door. "I might as well tell you now so that you can be prepared for this ordeal. They're a bit more lively than your puppet." A growing din was heard emerging from the kitchen. He peered over her shoulder. "I believe they've decided to surprise you and use the dishwasher. I'm not sure they know how to work it properly."

Kate whirled around and headed toward the kitchen double time.

"See you tonight," Bryan called. "I hope," he added as he shut the door behind him.

Chapter Five

The saleswoman looked a little uneasy as four seemingly identical little boys converged before her from two different directions. She glanced incredulously at Kate. "Are they yours?"

"Mine," Kate confirmed. She took hold of Trevor's hand and beckoned the others to stand by her.

The saleswoman was obviously appraising her. It was clear by the expression on the older woman's carefully made-up face that she regarded Kate as having one too many birds on her antenna.

She looked at the boys. "How do you manage?"

"Mike, please bring Trent back," she instructed as the younger boy suddenly disappeared into the circular clothes rack. Kate looked at the saleswoman. She saw no reason to tell the presumptuous woman that the boys weren't her children, just her charges. "Quite well, thank you."

Mike dragged back a protesting Trent. Travis

started to dash over to them to help rescue his mirror image. Kate very calmly caught him by the shoulder before he could get going. Travis looked up at Kate, frustrated. Kate merely shook her head. Travis shrugged and calmed down.

"So I see. Quads?"

"Triplets and a dividend," Kate replied.

Mike beamed and preened before his siblings.

Kate suppressed a smile as she pretended not to notice. "I thought it might save time if I gave you this list of things I need for the boys."

The saleswoman smiled for the first time as Kate removed the list from her purse. It was extensive. Having made a quick inventory at home, Kate had discovered that there were quite a few things the last housekeeper had neglected to get for the boys.

"Are they going away?" the woman asked, instantly more solicitous. A commission was, after all, a commission.

Kate thought of the color-coded, easy-identification system she had come up with this morning. "No, just finally coming into their own."

The statement was incomprehensible to the woman, but the list was not. "If you'll just follow me." She began to lead the way into a brightly decorated area of the young boys' department. Miniature dummies with pale complexions and expensive clothes stood all around them.

"Now I have very definite ideas about the colors I want," Kate told the woman.

The saleswoman turned, giving Kate her broadest smile. "Yes, yes, of course." She stopped before a rack of slacks. The boys fanned out in three different directions—except for Trevor, who stayed close to Kate, watching.

"Now these are very sturdy," the woman told Kate, taking out a leading name-brand pair of pants and holding them up for her inspection.

"Kate!"

Kate knew enough not to ignore a cry of that timbre. She turned toward Trevor, then looked in the direction he was pointing. She arrived at the tottering dummy in time to keep it from toppling down on Travis's head. The saleswoman gasped.

Travis looked up at her with a guilty expression on his face. "I'm sorry I did that, Kate," he mumbled.

Kate righted the mannequin. "I'm sure you are." She put out her hand. Travis looked down at it for a moment before taking it. "Come stand by me, Travis, and give me your opinion." She drew him back to the saleswoman, who was now looking at the group with a good deal of apprehension on her face. She stood out of range of any display mannequins.

Travis scratched his head with his free hand. "What's a 'pinyon?"

"*Oh*-pinyon, dummy," Mike injected, giving him a slight shove. All it took was a reproving look from Kate to make him drop his hand to his side.

"No, Mike, the dummy's the one that almost fell over. This is your brother." Kate's voice was kindly, but her message was quite clear. Mike nodded ruefully. She smiled and looked back at Travis. "An opinion is what you think of something."

"Can I give mine?" Trent cried eagerly, not wanting to be left out.

"No, me. Me." Trevor tried to edge his way ahead

of his two brothers. An elbow met his chest. He winced and stepped back.

Gently but firmly, Kate drew Trevor back to her. He flashed her an appreciative grin. "You'll all have a chance to give your opinions," Kate informed them. "But I won't be asking the opinions of little boys who are too busy fighting to talk."

The boys all exchanged looks, silently conferring as only children so close in age could. And then they quietly retreated two to each side of her. The saleswoman looked at Kate with new respect.

"Listen, I've got two kids at home who are absolute hellions. Do you give lessons?"

Trevor apparently didn't understand the nature of the woman's question, but he appeared threatened. He grabbed Kate's hand and hugged it to him. "No, she's ours."

"That I am, Trevor." Carefully she extricated her hand. "I'll take eight of those," she pointed, "two per boy. Now, about the colors—"

Bryan looked impatiently at the digital clock in his car. Six-fifteen. He had been on the road for over an hour. Ridiculous when he considered that his office was only thirty miles from home. Normally he could put up with the traffic snarls that occurred on the freeway. But tonight was different. He had hoped to be on time on Kate's first full day. He didn't want her to think that this was the way things were going to be, that he would be late getting in every night. He had promised that she'd have time to study. He didn't want her to think that it was a lie. And, if this morning was any indication, the boys were already comfortable enough with her to be themselves. By now she was undoubtedly at her wit's end. It wasn't fair to prolong her agony this early in the game.

If she was even there.

Bryan banished the thought from his mind. She wasn't the type to just leave them alone. He didn't know why he trusted her so much, but he knew he did. It was a feeling he had about her.

Yeah, like the feeling you had about Jill, remember? You're not exactly the world's hottest judge of character.

He blocked out the mocking voice and the memory it dredged up. With Jill it had been a personal judgment. Kate was strictly a professional matter. The two had no connection.

As if to call him a liar, an image of Kate, standing on a chair and reaching into her closet flashed in his mind's eye. Long, tanned legs that made his hands itch were particularly featured.

He tightened them around the steering wheel and forced himself to remember that she was his sons' governess and only that. He looked at the clock again. *If* she still wanted the job after tonight. She probably didn't bargain on spending so much time alone with them.

Well, he hadn't bargained on this much traffic.

The automobiles in front of him moved like bumper cars on a game board, an inch at a time. There was nothing he could do but wait. Unless...

He picked up his car phone and dialed. Why hadn't he thought of that before? What was wrong with him lately? One. Two. Three rings. No answer. Maybe she sold them and then ran off. Four rings. Now he was getting concerned. Five—

"Hello?"

She sounded breathless. Were they giving her that hard a time?

"Kate?"

"Yes?"

He heard noise in the background. He began to relax. "This is Bryan Marlowe."

"Oh, hello, Mr. Marlowe."

"Are you all right?"

"Yes, why shouldn't I be?" What an odd question, she thought. The man was a definite worrier, even if he didn't look like the type.

"You sound breathless."

"Oh, that." She laughed. "We were playing tag. I was 'it' when the phone rang."

Her laugh made him itchy. Itchy in an old, familiar way that he hadn't thought about in two years. "Then everything's all right?"

"Well, not everything."

He knew it. "Why, what's wrong?"

"Dinner is getting very dry in the oven. How soon will you be home?"

He almost laughed in relief. "As soon as the cars start to move again. I'm stuck in traffic." He watched a car try to cut in front of another, using two feet of space. California drivers never ceased to amaze him.

She liked the sound of his voice on the telephone. It was low and sexy. Fine thoughts to be having about your employer, Kate, she chided herself, then smiled.

Fine thoughts indeed. "Traffic. Is that what I hear in the background?"

"Yes." A shriek echoed in the phone. Not hers. "What is it *I* hear in the background?"

Kate looked behind her. Tag was over. Cowboys and Indians was now the game of choice. And there was a lasso coming at her. She stepped out of the way just in time. "Yours sons, about to lasso me, it seems."

He muttered under his breath. Why couldn't they behave themselves? "I'll be there as soon as I can," he promised. Cradling the receiver against his neck, he found himself trying to cut ahead using the same trick the other car had just employed.

Necessity was the mother of invention all right, he thought as he made it. He looked up in his rearview mirror and saw the driver behind him glaring.

"Have a desire to rescue a damsel in distress, do you?"

Her words were not what he expected. Panic was what he expected, not humor and certainly not that warm, sensual tone. "Yes, if that damsel's in my employ."

"Ah, you're a born romantic, you are, Mr. Marlowe." There was a low chuckle before she said goodbye and hung up.

Bryan stared at the receiver. Now what did that mean? He was beginning to think that Kate was sending out some very enigmatic signals. Well, it didn't matter what her signals meant. At this point in his life, he couldn't handle any additional complications.

Impatient to get home, he stepped on the gas and moved up three feet.

* * *

She wasn't in the living room. Neither were the boys. And the house was unnaturally quiet. Bryan's concern increased as he hurried toward the stairs.

From the corner of his eye, he glanced at the kitchen, then stopped short. His sons were sitting at the table. Quietly. He wondered if she had somehow gotten her hands on a tranquilizer gun.

Bryan walked toward the kitchen like a man in a trance.

Not only were his sons quiet, they were neat and dressed in new clothes. Each of the boys was wearing a matching shirt and pants. And each wore a different color from his brothers. The place settings in front of them matched their shirts. It looked like a scene from an early fifties family musical.

Coming to, Bryan looked around for Kate. She was at the stove, dishing out peas into a serving bowl. She smiled a greeting.

"You're home." The word "finally" was silent, but definitely implied.

But he was too awestruck to take exception at her tone. He stared at his sons, and then at her. "They're color-coordinated," he said needlessly.

"Yes," she replied mildly, setting the peas on the table, "they are. Eat up, boys." Four sets of hands went out for the spoon that was in the bowl of peas. "Clockwise," she advised, "starting with Mike."

Mike looked triumphant as he claimed the spoon.

They didn't even *like* peas, Bryan marveled. What had she *done* to them?

"You're just in time for dinner, Mr. Marlowe." She turned back to the stove. "Ten more minutes and it would have been dry enough to use as shoe leather.'' Kate removed the casserole dish from the oven with mittened hands.

Bryan dropped his attaché case on the floor beside his chair. He loosened his tie, feeling the need to. "Why?" he wanted to know.

Kate arranged the hot dish in the center of the table. "Because chicken tetrazzini can only stay in the oven for so long before drying out."

"Hang the chicken—"

Deftly she began ladling out a portion on Mike's dish and then continued serving clockwise around the table, just as she had instructed the boys. "Hang the chicken, Mr. Marlowe? Did it ever do anything to you?" She exchanged glances with the boys, who broke out in a series of giggles. She shook her head to quiet them, but it was evident that she shared their amusement.

Where had all this camaraderie come from? She had only been here a day. "I mean, why are my sons color coordinated?"

He certainly became annoyed easily, she thought. Stress, she decided. The man needed to learn how to relax. She would make it her duty to teach him.

In a soothing voice, she explained, "It simplifies things. I can almost always tell them apart without using any gimmicks. But if they move fast, it does make things more difficult. This way, I know at a glance who didn't pick up his clothes, who didn't eat his carrots—"

"Carrots?" Trent moaned, sticking out his tongue. "Yuck."

"Tomorrow night," Kate said in an aside. "We'll

handle that later." She turned her attention to Bryan. "You don't approve?"

He made himself comfortable at the table. "Yes, I only wish I had thought of it myself."

"I'm sure you would have," she said with a smile, "in time."

It was a nice smile, he thought. He could see the boys vying for it. "Blarney, Ms. Llewellyn."

"Diplomacy, Mr. Marlowe." She surveyed the progress the boys were making with their meal. "Eat, boys. It's good for you."

He looked at dinner for the first time. "Tetrazzini, did you say?"

Kate nodded, then watched with pleasure as Bryan helped himself to a good-sized serving.

He noted the way the boys were eating. They were actually enjoying the meal. "How did you talk them out of hot dogs? That's what they usually ask for for dinner."

"The subject," Kate told him pleasantly, "never came up."

And if it had, Bryan thought as he began to eat, she would have found a way to talk them out of it. He was beginning to feel that he had made the right choice after all.

At least for his sons.

It was later that evening, and he had settled down to do some work he had brought home with him. The boys had gone off to bed a full hour ago. To his surprise and relief, he didn't hear the sound of running feet coming his way. The boys almost always found some excuse to come into the den to talk to him even after he tucked them in. Anything rather than go to bed.

Tonight, though, it was quiet. He caught himself smiling. He could get used to that.

Bryan was midway through his research when he had the feeling that he was being watched. He looked up and saw her standing in the doorway. She was leaning against the jamb, her arms folded before her chest, her hair loose and flowing about her shoulders. She looked just the way she had at dinner.

So why was she now arousing feelings in him that had to stay dormant if this situation was to work?

Because she had aroused those feelings earlier, too, but then he had been too awestruck by his sons to pay close attention to his own needs.

He blocked them out now.

"You were busy," she explained, seeing the question in his eyes. "I was waiting for an opening. I thought you might want to know how today went."

"Yes, I would. Come in." He gestured for her to come in, then noticed that she was looking at him intently and making no effort to hide it. "What are you staring at?"

She sat down on the sofa that was placed before the fireplace. It was the first piece of furniture he had ever purchased, and he was appallingly sentimental about it. Kate put her hand on the corner and leaned into it. "You have a dimple. I never noticed it before."

The observation seemed much too personal, and he found himself shying away from it. "I'm working on having it become a frown line. Trial lawyers with dimples don't strike fear into the hearts of their opponents."

She cocked her head, still studying him. "Is that what you want to do, strike fear?" Somehow, she didn't believe it, even if he thought he did.

He leaned back in his swivel chair and arched a brow. "Are you practicing your psych lessons on me?"

Kate laughed softly. He looked uneasy again, she thought, and wished he wouldn't. "Hardly. I'm a child-psychology major. I think you're a little too old to fall into that category." She backed away from the subject. There would be time enough later to find out why he felt the need to be so guarded. Kate brushed her hair back from her forehead. "The boys are asleep."

"Thank God," he muttered. Tonight he didn't have the strength for arguments or disputes.

Kate saw through his words. "You love them a lot, don't you?" She leaned her chin on her hands and looked up at him.

When she did that, she looked a lot sexier than any governess had a right to be, he thought. "Why? Didn't my sigh of relief sound convincing enough?"

"No." Her smile spread as a fond memory came back to her. "My mother used to sigh just that way when she finally got the wee ones off to bed."

Without realizing how effortlessly it had happened, he found himself slipping into Kate's world. "How many 'wee ones' of you were there?"

"Eleven altogether."

He whistled. "I don't feel so bad now."

"Neither did she."

"Eleven children," he repeated, marveling. Even though he dearly loved his sons, he couldn't even begin to imagine life with eleven children. "How the hell did your mother manage?"

"With a firm hand and a lot of love."

He was more of a realist than that. "And very little sleep."

"Not a wink in twenty years." Kate laughed fondly.

"Remarkable woman."

"I always thought so."

He thought of dinner earlier and how well behaved his sons had been. "It seems to have rubbed off."

Kate shrugged off the compliment carelessly. "A little of it had to seep in, but I'm far from remarkable, just patient."

"With four energetic boys, that in itself is remarkable."

"I haven't been here that long, but I haven't noticed you lose your temper with them."

He shifted a bit uncomfortably, and Kate could have sworn he stiffened. Why? It struck her as an odd reaction. "I have a lot to make up to them."

"Being both mother and father?" she guessed.

He looked back at his paperwork. He moved papers around without really seeing them. "Something like that," he muttered evasively.

Kate rose, watching him. What had changed his tone? She moved closer, stopping next to his desk. "They do miss her a lot."

He cleared his throat. "It's only natural. But they were very young when she died. They don't remember that much." His voice was curt.

Kate took it as a dismissal of the subject, although it gave her insight. Bryan's wound seemed to be very raw, as if his wife's death had just happened. It was unusual to grieve for such a long time. Their marriage, she decided, must have been something special.

"Well, I'd better get back and do the dishes."

Bryan said nothing as she left, then felt guilty at the way he had treated her. Here she came, practically a miracle worker, taming his unruly sons in a little over twenty-four hours, and he was biting her head off.

He walked into the kitchen and found her washing the dinner dishes that were still piled up in the sink.

"You don't have to do that," Bryan told her. "You can just stack them in the dishwasher." He wanted to apologize, but the words didn't form in his mouth. The circumstances of Jill's death were too painful for him to discuss with a relative stranger, even a very sympathetic one. It was his own private hell to carry around with him.

"I know," Kate answered brightly. "But I like the feel of cleaning things. It's a curse, I'm afraid."

"Not around here it's not." Bryan felt the tension within him easing. "If that's your hobby, you'll find plenty to make you happy here. That was one of the reasons one of the last housekeepers quit. Too much to clean." Without thinking, he picked up a dish towel. Kate grinned and handed him the dish she had just washed. "That's why I finally decided to split this job."

Kate stopped washing. Water continued to run over her hands. "I beg your pardon?"

"The house and the boys are too much for one

woman to handle." He stopped. Unconsciously his words triggered a memory of Jill saying the very same thing.

Kate saw the faraway, sad look in his eyes. "Mr. Marlowe? Mr. Marlowe, are you all right?"

"Hmm? Oh yes, I was just..." He paused. "Thinking," he finally said.

And it hurt, Kate thought. She felt for him, but there wasn't anything she could do—yet. Not if he didn't want her to. The best she could do was to change the subject. "You were saying about splitting the job?"

"Yes, I want to hire a regular housekeeper, as well. It'll be easier finding one now that my main, um, difficulty—" they both smiled at his reference "—is taken care of. She'll take care of all the household chores. I just want you to concern yourself with the boys, exclusively."

Not exclusively, Mr. Marlowe. I think you need some looking after, too. "I don't mind helping out. I enjoy hard work."

"You're a rare woman, Kate."

"Flattery will get you everywhere, Mr. Marlowe. I hope you hold that thought when you find the bills."

"Bills?"

"For the boys' clothes and accessories. I have them in my room." She turned off the water. "I can go get them now if—"

He shook his head. "No need. I gave you carte blanche. So far, I'm not disappointed. Do whatever you need to do." He picked up the next dish and began wiping. He appeared preoccupied again.

Kate turned on the water once more, searching for

the next dish. "I fully intend to, Mr. Marlowe. I fully intend to."

Bryan had no idea why it sounded like a well-intended threat. "Oh, one more thing."

"Yes?"

He felt as if he were asking her to be a sacrificial lamb, but there was no getting around it. "The boys need to go to the dentist for a checkup. The last housekeeper—"

"Was afraid," Kate concluded, remembering his reference to the shopping trip. "Certainly was a mousy little thing, wasn't she?"

"Not when she first came here," Bryan assured her.

"I'll handle it."

He had no doubt that she would.

Chapter Six

For almost a week, the Marlowe household had been, in a manner of speaking, turned inside out. Chaos had become order, cacophony had yielded to the mellow hum of an agreeable family. Bryan had stood back, absorbing it all in disbelief. He was amazed at Kate's control over the boys. Yet there was an element of doubt gnawing at his mind. Kate was unique, had affected him uniquely and, obviously on a different level, had affected his sons. Affected them, yes; changed them, no. It wasn't possible. He doubted that anything could change them. This unexpected behavior was unnatural. An enormous amount of energy and mischievousness was being bottled up. Visions of a corked, agitated bottle of champagne stood before his mind's eye. The quiet calm enveloping the house gave no indication of the inevitable explosion that he was sure would take place. Contentment began to give way to a sense of foreboding.

Monday morning seemed to herald in the inevitable explosion. The morning had begun innocuously enough at breakfast with a discussion of what was to transpire after school. Kate had precipitated it by uttering the dreaded word that brought dismay to young and old alike: *dentist.*

"All right, boys," she said briskly as she put away a carton of milk into the refrigerator, "today after school we're all going to the dentist. Your father tells me that you're way overdue. I made an appointment for all of you with Dr. Flores."

The boys, lined up behind her with their breakfast dishes, looked stunned and betrayed. A chorus of moans met her words.

Bryan gulped the remainder of his coffee. This would be a good time to beat a hasty retreat to his car. He was sure Kate wouldn't want him to see her embroiled in a losing battle. This very probably would be the beginning of the end of her reign of peace. He felt she deserved to be left alone at this moment of ignominious defeat.

"What's the matter, Mike?" Kate accepted the dish from his outstretched hand and placed it into the sink. The action was repeated with each boy in turn.

"We don't want to go." Mike jutted out his lower lip and folded his arms across his chest like a disgruntled old Indian chief. Travis aped his older brother.

Kate stopped and pretended to consider the six-year-old's protest. "Why?"

"We don't like the dentist," Trent put in.

"Why?" she repeated.

"'Cause." Travis uttered the single word as if it were a detailed explanation.

Kate looked at Trevor, but the boy said nothing. He appeared very uncertain. He didn't know her well enough to feel comfortable about taking a stand in this matter.

She shook her head. "'Fraid you'll have to do better than that if you expect me to take your side."

Bryan stopped at the front door, intrigued. He knew that if he didn't leave now, he'd be disastrously engulfed in morning traffic. But he wanted to see how she was going to resolve this. Quietly he slipped back to the kitchen doorway.

"You mean if we give you a good enough reason, we don't hafta go?" Mike's eyes opened so wide they threatened to fall out.

Kate spied Bryan watching her from the doorway, but pretended not to notice. "Seems fair."

"He hurts!" Trent cried out. Kate gave him a very penetrating look. Trent retreated. "Well, maybe not so much," he amended in a smaller voice.

"I'm sure he hurts a little." Trent flashed her a relieved grin that faded with her next words. "But cavities hurt more. They give you toothaches. The dentist stops them before they get the best of you." She looked at the others. "Anyone else?"

Trevor mumbled something into his chin.

"What?" She leaned her head toward him. "Speak up, Trevor. I'm afraid that your brothers have louder voices than you."

Trevor stood on his toes, as if that would help his voice carry better. "I said, I guess that means we're going."

"Well, yes, I suppose it does at that. But think of it as making sure you have big, strong healthy teeth to smile with." She ran her finger down his nose affectionately. The boy smiled in response. Kate held up her hands in front of her face and took a step back. "Stop, you're blinding me."

As if on cue, the boys all gathered around her, grinning as broadly as they could. Kate laughed. She should have known they'd do this. But it was better to have them in a giddy mood than having to fight four stubborn boys who refused to go to the dentist.

The foreseen explosion did not materialize. Bryan was amazed and not a little impressed.

Over their heads, she saw Bryan still watching her. He inclined his head slightly in approval. She understood the gesture and accepted the compliment with a smile and a wink.

She saw the startled look on his face. She hadn't meant to wink, it had just happened. When she was around him, he brought out very basic feelings within her, like the need for a human being to touch another. And maybe just a little more. Had he read her feelings? Was that why he looked so surprised? she wondered. The look in his own eyes turned darker, but not the dark of anger. The dark of emotions kept suppressed. He seemed to be responding by absorbing all of her with those smoldering gray eyes of his. A slight, involuntary shudder passed over her.

Was she as spontaneous and warm with a man as she was with children? The thought burst upon him without warning, startling Bryan just as her wink had. He cut it short. Whatever she was like in the company of others, including men, was no concern of his. He needed her as a nursemaid, a baby-sitter, that was all. The way she was with his sons was what mattered, nothing else, not the softness of her skin, or the quick way her smile reached her eyes or the supple way she moved. None of this should be of interest to him.

So why was it?

He had no desire to become involved with another woman, no desire to let another woman hurt him. The best way to insure this was to remain detached. He had to maintain his control, his composure. His feelings had remained contained behind an impregnable wall for two years. Yet, with no more than a smile, a facial expression, a simple touch, Kate had caused cracks to form in his emotional fortress. The woman was dangerous to his very self-preservation.

Bryan slowly turned toward the front door, fully absorbed with his thoughts. "Good luck," he called out more to Kate than the boys. "I might be late coming home." He knew that he would be, on purpose. He wanted to be around her, and he had to put a stop to that. He needed to put more space between them to properly reaffirm his hold on things.

"We'll be here," Kate called back. She turned her attention to the boys. "All right, my fine young lads, it's off to school with the lot of you. Hurry now, or we'll be late."

Snacks had already been packed and tucked into color-coordinated backpacks earlier that morning. They were lined up neatly in a row on the living-room sofa nearest the door. Each boy grabbed the right pack. There was no fighting over possessions, no accusations or fists hurtling through the air.

Bryan took in this demonstration of harmony before he left the house. God, how had he ever lived without this woman?

Dangerous thought, he warned himself. He couldn't grow dependent on her—for many reasons.

"See you boys tonight."

A chorus of soprano goodbyes followed him in his wake. Bryan walked to his car, marveling. Kate had done more in a handful of days to institute order than all the other housekeepers combined had done during their entire stays. Up until now, he had been the only one who was able to make the boys behave, and even that only lasted for as long as he was physically present. As soon as he was at work or away, the boys did as they very well pleased. Now it appeared that the boys had met their match in a spirited, blue-eyed blonde who wasn't all that much taller than they were. Five feet, if he stretched it.

Something within him wanted to stretch that frame taut against his body.

He caught a glimpse of his expression in the rear-view mirror. He was smiling. Broadly. The corners around his mouth were soft. He adjusted his mirror to its proper position.

Damn, what was coming over him?

It was only because he knew he didn't have to worry so much about the boys anymore, he told himself. Yet the stirrings of his body told him differently, and he was beginning to realize that he was going to have to acknowledge it for what it was.

Okay, so she was attractive. Compared to the last housekeeper, the Bride of Frankenstein would have been attractive, he thought as he pulled into the stream of traffic flowing on the avenue. And maybe he was attracted to her. Slightly. So he wasn't entirely dead, so what did that prove, exactly? That he had a few male hormones left? Wanton things, hormones. They led one into difficult situations.

A car pulled out of a driveway and darted in front of him. Bryan braked too hard. His body jolted to reenforce the jolt his mind just felt. He had just admitted to being attracted to Kate. He hadn't been attracted to any woman since Jill had died.

It had to stop right there.

He wasn't home at six. Or at seven. For several hours afterward, he kept finding things to do that kept him at the office. He stopped suddenly, assessing his actions. This was ridiculous. Why should he be afraid to go home? He *lived* there. His *sons* lived there. What was he afraid of confronting?

His own vulnerability, a small voice echoed.

Making the same mistake, it added. Twice.

"Planning on burning the midnight oil, Marlowe?" Angus Hitchcock, a wizen old gentleman whose name was the first one etched on the firm's outer door peered into the book-lined room. "Everyone else has gone home, you know."

"You haven't," Bryan pointed out.

Angus walked in. He crossed to the chair next to Bryan's desk and slowly lowered his gaunt frame into it. "I've no one to go home to. You've those sons of yours." Bushy white eyebrows with flecks of gray drew together as he studied Bryan's face. "By the way, how's the new woman turning out?"

The term disturbed Bryan. That was the whole problem. He kept thinking of Kate as a woman, not just as an employee, which is, after all, just what she was. Just like Mrs. Woolsey had been.

A wry smile slipped over his lips. Well, maybe not just like Mrs. Woolsey.

He was aware that Angus was waiting for an answer. "She appears to be doing rather well. The boys seem to adore her. Even Trevor."

Angus nodded his head thoughtfully. With his mane of thick, snow-white hair, he looked a little like a wise old lion. "How is the boy? Any better?"

Bryan put aside his stack of papers. "Still doesn't talk very much. I know that the doctor said it just takes time, but it's been two years. You'd think he'd come around."

"You'd think so, wouldn't you?" Hitchcock gave his junior partner a long, hard look that saw too much. "But then, look at his father."

Bryan had come to regard Angus as almost a father figure. The man was sharp and he was fair. But that still didn't allow Bryan to accept his observation any less grudgingly. His manner grew more formal. "I win all my cases in court, Angus. That's all that counts."

Angus put his gnarled hand on the desk and leaned heavily on it as he rose to his feet again. "If you think that, you're a lot less intelligent than I gave you credit for."

Bryan pushed his chair back and got up. He snapped his attaché closed, his expression unreadable. "You're right, Angus. It is getting late." He crossed to the door. "I'll see you in the morning."

Angus stood looking after his junior partner and silently shook his head.

* * *

It was nearly eleven when he finally got home. Bryan had expected to hunt up a sandwich from the refrigerator and see about getting a good night's sleep after checking on his sons. In the last week, Kate had been successful in instituting the one thing even he had never been able to enforce. A bedtime. It was now way past the boys', and he was fully prepared to find them in bed and the house quiet. He looked forward to being alone for a change.

His expectations were fulfilled on two counts: his sons were asleep and the house was quiet. But he wasn't alone. When he walked into the kitchen for his sandwich, he found Kate sitting at the table, studying. He knew she was waiting up for him. Something jumped within his stomach when she looked up and smiled at him.

"I was just about to send the bloodhounds out after you."

"Shawn?"

She thought of the puppet she had used to entertain the boys before they went to bed tonight. "No, he wouldn't be much good, I'm afraid." She touched her nose. "Can't smell anything." She got up and crossed over to him. "Probably has something to do with his being related to a sock."

"Probably."

She smiled up at his face as she took his arm and led him to the table. He felt a strong urge to bend his head and kiss her. He fought it.

"You look tired," she observed.

He didn't want her concern, didn't want her kindness. It led to other things, things that had no place in his life anymore. "This is the way I usually look at eleven."

She perceived a note of irritation. "And waspish," she added to her observation.

He removed his arm from her grasp. Her close proximity was making him nervous inside, threatening to undo him, taunting him with the fact that he wanted her in his arms. "I am not waspish."

She smiled her denial of his denial. "Definitely waspish. Probably because you've had no dinner."

Why wasn't she asleep? Just his luck to be sharing his house with someone who never slept. Probably took after her mother. "I sent out for a sandwich at six."

Kate just shook her head. "Mighty poor substitute for nourishment, that. C'mon—" she motioned toward his chair and then busied herself at the oven "—I've kept supper waiting for you."

He looked in the general direction of the stairs. "I should look in on the boys."

"They've been sound asleep for the past two hours."

"No requests for glasses of water?"

"None."

He shook his head. "I just might have you canonized." He eyed the plate of food that Kate put down at his place. It'd serve no purpose not to eat it. Bryan sat down. "Speaking of miracles, how did the trip to the dentist go?"

"Wonderful!" she enthused. Kate joined him at the table. She pushed her books aside and rested her elbow on the table as she nursed a mug of coffee. "None of them had cavities." She leaned forward confidentially. "I don't mind telling you, I did sweat a little over the verdict until it came in. I would have hated having led one of those trusting little souls into a dentist's chair to be drilled on."

"Those 'trusting little souls' bit the last house-keeper who tried to take them to the dentist. I'm still not sure how you managed to pull it off." Yes I am. You're part witch.

The glow from the overhead kitchen light seemed to play on her lips. No lipstick, yet they looked moist and inviting. Bryan forced himself to look down at the slice of Virginia ham on his plate. Mechanically he began to cut it.

"Nothing to it, really. Just a little child psychology."

"Oh, I forgot, your major."

"Yes—" pugnaciously she leaned her head on one fisted hand "—and I'm darn good at it."

Her eyes were smiling, even though she was attempting to maintain a straight face.

He couldn't resist her tone. "You won't hear any dispute from me. As a matter of fact, I'd say you deserve a raise."

"Well, I won't be giving you an argument over that idea." She tapped his as yet unsampled dinner. "Now eat."

How could she sound so motherly and look so damn sexy at the same time? He felt attraction stirring, hard and demanding, and he became defensive. "I'm not one of the boys, Kate."

She heard the warning note in his voice. Stubbornly she disregarded it. "Well, not chronologically, but no one's so old that they can't stand for another human being to care for their needs.''

"My needs are well cared for."

Bryan's stomach chose to join her side. There was a low, rumbling sound, testifying to his hunger.

The grin she wore was one of triumph. Being an astute lawyer, Bryan knew he had lost the round. "Eat your dinner, Mr. Marlowe," she said sweetly. "One of your needs is making itself known."

He took a bite grudgingly. A whiz at painless disciplining and a terrific cook, too. The woman was just too good to be true, and he knew that was a fact. Things were never quite what they seemed. "Are you always right?" he asked archly after he had swallowed another mouthful.

The question surprised her. Was that a tinge of resentment she heard? It didn't make sense. "Aren't you paying me for that?"

"I thought I was paying you to watch over my sons."

They were sparring, and Kate didn't exactly understand why or what about, but she was determined to somehow hold her own. "My mother always said I did more than was asked of me."

"Did your mother ever find a way to make you toe the line?"

"Not that I remember."

"I didn't think so."

Despite an intense need to the contrary, he couldn't help smiling. Maybe she was contagious. She certainly smiled enough. Kate was warm, extroverted, creative, enthusiastic, impractical, and had a wonderful sense of humor. Effective, yet unpredictable. A grab bag of pleasant surprises. He couldn't remember when someone had kept dinner waiting for him for four hours. Certainly not a housekeeper. But then, this was no ordinary housekeeper. All in all, Ms. Katherine Llewellyn was a very intriguing package, even to a man who didn't want to be intrigued.

"Good?" Kate indicated his almost-empty plate.

"Good," he acknowledged.

"Good." She was content just to sit there with silence as their companion.

The silence made him more uneasy than her conversation. "Don't you have anything to study?"

"Yes. You."

He cleared his throat. "I meant books."

She glanced at the stack at her left. "I did all my work, waiting for you to come home."

"You didn't have to wait up," he said gruffly.

"Oh, but I did. I couldn't just go to bed, knowing you'd be coming home to a quiet house."

He put down his knife and fork. "Did it ever occur to you that I might like a quiet house? That I might actually *long* for a quiet house?"

He thought he had her there, but she turned the tables on him. "If you did, then you'd have sent the boys away to boarding school."

She understood him too well for his own damn good, he thought. He moved his chair a little until it was closer to hers. He put his hand on the back of it. "You have a very stubborn streak, you know that?"

"Yes, I have." Kate grew warm as anticipation and hope built.

He should be getting up. He should be walking

away. His knees wouldn't move. "Proud of it, I take it."

"Very."

Maybe it was the way her lips moved when they formed the word "very." Maybe she had drugged the ham. Or maybe he had been without a woman for so long, he didn't have the strength to fight the feeling that was growing within him. Desire, hot and demanding, pulsated through him. He leaned toward her. She didn't move. She was waiting. He filled his hands with her hair, framing her face. He felt both strong and weak, both in control and swept away.

He felt that if he didn't kiss her now, he was going to explode.

"Are you studying my head to make a sculpture, or are you planning to kiss me?" The words would have been teasing if they hadn't been so softly spoken.

"Kiss you."

"Then get on with it. Please."

His breath was on her face and it caused her to flutter her lashes.

"You do talk too much," he told her.

"Aye, there is that."

And then he silenced her in the most effective way he knew how. Closed her mouth to words and opened a door that he thought had permanently slammed shut within him.

Promises were usually empty. He had learned that long ago. And yet the promise of her lips was not empty. The kiss he found there gave him so much more than he had even remotely expected.

God, she felt wonderful. He pulled her to him, cup-

ping her head now with one hand while the other
pulled her toward him. Despite his three-piece suit,
he felt her soft breasts press against him. He knew he
would have felt them even if he had been wearing a
suit of armor. There were things about this woman
that branded him, that seared their way into his soul
no matter how much he tried to guard against them.

His mouth moved over hers, raising all sorts of
demands he knew should not, *could* not be met.

Kate felt no hesitancy. This felt right, *was* right.
Her hands slid up his back, her fingers curving as if
to anchor her to him. Her head spun even as the room
ebbed away.

One kiss and things would never be the same again,
she thought. Thank God.

But it was over too soon, much too soon. She felt
him withdraw. Reluctantly she let her hands drop
from his back and opened her eyes. She saw pain in
his. Pain and anger. Why?

"You do take a girl's breath away," she whispered.

"I'm sorry. I shouldn't have done that."

The words hurt. He wasn't supposed to be sorry,
not for kissing her. But she kept her feelings to herself. "Why?"

"Because."

Like sons, like father. "You'll have to do better
than that if you expect me to be taking your side."

"That's what you said to the boys this morning."

"Seems to fit here, too." She drew a breath, trying
desperately to understand what was troubling him.
"There's no harm in a simple kiss, Mr. Marlowe."
He was Mr. Marlowe again, not Bryan, not the man

who had kissed her. "One human being reaching out to another. Happens a lot in the real world."

"I know all about the real world, Kate."

He stepped away, forcing back the desire to once again take her into his arms. He knew that way lay only trouble, and he had had enough of trouble. And he had no right to cause her any hardship.

"Dinner was very good. Now, if you'll excuse me," he picked up his attaché case, "I have work to do."

"You can run," she whispered to herself, taking his plate to the sink, "but you can't hide. You've a bleeding heart, Mr. Bryan Marlowe, and I can't stand to see anything hurting. Not even a man who doesn't want help."

She turned the water on in the sink and unconsciously ran her fingertips along her mouth. The imprint of his kiss was still there.

Chapter Seven

Kate knocked twice on the closed bedroom door. "Mr. Marlowe?"

Bryan was just coming out of the shower. Her voice startled him. Always an early riser, Bryan had gotten a late start that morning. It was because of her. He had lain awake for half the night, trying to think about work, about the boys, about anything except what was really on his mind. His efforts had been fruitless. Images of Kate kept bursting upon his brain with the regularity of a pulse no matter where he tried to direct his thoughts. The moment they had shared in a passion-filled embrace kept replaying itself for him until he was convinced that he had regressed to an adolescent boy relishing his first interlude.

Just as he had resigned himself to a totally sleepless night, he had dozed off. But she had been there, too, in his dreams. Plaguing him, making him want things, making him remember life as it had been, or rather, as he had once imagined it might be.

He awoke more tired than when he had gone to bed. To make matters worse, he had overslept by an hour. While rushing through his shower, he couldn't help wondering what their first encounter after last night would be like. He hadn't imagined he'd be facing it dressed in only a towel.

Because there seemed to be an urgent note in her voice, he opened the door quickly. His first thought was that someone had gotten hurt.

"I—" Kate stopped, her gaze involuntarily surveying the muscular, slightly damp body before her. Drops of water still clung to the light swirl of dark hair on his chest. What had seemed so important just a few seconds ago melted away as a warm, sensuous feeling spread through her.

She suddenly realized that she wasn't breathing in enough air. She felt flushed, yet not embarrassed, as a smile curved her lips.

He looked good. No, actually, he was almost magnificent. Kate took a deep breath and then made light of the situation, recognizing that they both needed the ruse. "Aren't you a little under-dressed for the weather, Mr. Marlowe?"

He gripped the towel that was slipping from his waist and pressed it against his hip. It made him look, Kate thought, indescribably delicious.

He realized, too late, that in his unsettled state he had mistakenly perceived urgency in her voice. She had merely been rushing around as she was prone to do. Now, standing there like this in front of her, his nerves were reacting to another emergency entirely, a need to give in to the desperate urges that were demanding release. It took everything he had to deny himself.

He fumbled for words, hating the state he found himself in. "I thought that something was wrong... and I got a late start this morning. You called when I was coming out of the shower."

"Lucky for us you remembered to pick up a towel on the way."

He ignored the smile in her voice. "So, what's on your mind?"

You wouldn't want to know, she thought. Eyes back in your head, Katie me girl, she chided herself. It's only a man for all that. But Lord, what a man. She felt her pulse throb. It wasn't the only thing that throbbed. If this was God's way of testing her, she knew she was getting very low points for good behavior or purity of thought.

With effort, Kate maintained her composure as she leaned against the open door. "In the, um, excitement of last night—"

They exchanged looks, but neither commented. He gratefully accepted her tactfully worded reference to last night's events. His eyes skimmed over her face. She looked so warm and fresh. He felt an uncontrollable urge to take her into his arms and continue where they had left off last night.

He decided that he was going absolutely crazy.

"—I forgot to tell you that the agency sent over a list of women yesterday."

"What agency?" He grabbed his clothing from the bed, and his towel began to slip. With a deft hand, he caught it and made a hurried exit to the bathroom.

Kate followed him with her eyes, wishing her imagination wasn't quite so vivid.

"And what women?" he called out, hurrying into his trousers. "I didn't request any women. God knows," he said under his breath, "I've got my hands full with the one I've acquired."

She wasn't sure what he had mumbled to himself, so she answered only the first part. "Yes, you did."

Bryan came out, hastily tucking his shirttails into the waistband of his trousers. He stared at her as if she had just lapsed into a foreign language he couldn't follow. "When did I request women?"

Kate picked up his jacket and held it for him as he slid his arms in. "You said you wanted to hire a housekeeper, remember?"

He wished he knew what was going on behind those blue eyes. "No, I don't." He took his tie from the bureau and hurried down the steps. Today he'd have to skip breakfast no matter what this Irish sorceress might have to say to the contrary.

Kate was right behind him on the stairs and followed him into the living room. "Want to, or remember wanting to?"

"The latter."

He turned abruptly and she bumped into him. It caused a quick, combustible sensation he desperately wanted to explore, which was just why he couldn't.

For a moment, they looked into each other's eyes. Both saw needs, but only one of them pretended not to. Bryan cleared his throat.

"But you obviously did—remember, I mean. You're very efficient."

"You don't have time to take care of every little detail."

She was being too much of a helpmate. Too much like a wife, he thought. He knew he should resist the pleasant illusion that created, and yet he was finding it harder and harder to do just that.

And she had only been here a week. What would the future be like?

He was in trouble. Deep trouble.

"Now, then," Kate went on briskly, "when would be the best time?"

He was trying to remember when he had seen bluer eyes and to figure out why the color should disarm and affect him so much. "For what?"

Kate shook her head. "You're not paying attention, are you?"

He had the distinct impression that she was treating him just the way she treated the boys. He found himself wanting more from her than that. But why? He had told himself that he didn't want anything, remember? Maybe he wasn't paying attention to himself, either.

"No, I'm afraid I'm a little preoccupied this morning." *With petal-soft lips I had no business kissing.* He picked up his attaché case from its place on the hall table.

Gently Kate took it away again and set it down.

"Just what are you doing?"

She ushered him into the kitchen, where his sons were already sitting. "I thought it was evident. I'm taking away your attaché case and leading you to your breakfast."

"I haven't time for that."

"We'll discuss it while you eat," she promised.

He gave up and sat down. He felt too weary to put up a struggle. He knew he'd waste more time arguing with her than eating. She had taught him that, too, in the short time she had been here.

Kate contained the smile she felt forming. He was much too serious for her to be smiling, she thought. "All right, I'll take it from the top. The employment agency would like to know when would be the best time for you to hold interviews for the new housekeeper."

He was about to answer when he saw the startled look on his sons' faces.

Trevor upset his chair with a crash as he rushed over to Kate and grabbed hold of her hand. "Are you going away?"

Kate recognized fear in the small face. She crouched down so that he was spared having to look up at her. "No, honey. Your dad just wants me to have more time for you. A housekeeper will cook for you and clean up after you."

Trevor didn't seem completely convinced. He tightened his hold on her hand. "But you won't go away?"

"No, darling, I won't go away." She ruffled his hair. "And thank you."

He looked puzzled. "For what?"

"For making me feel wanted." She gave him a hug. "Everyone wants to feel wanted." She looked in Bryan's direction when she said it.

He wasn't certain if she was trying to analyze him or if she saw something that he was trying to hide from himself. He looked down at his plate and finished his bacon. He was doing this a lot, he realized: looking away to avoid her eyes. He wasn't a coward, wasn't used to running, but this feeling that seemed to be growing of its own accord, he had to admit, had him scared. It was best to keep contact with its source to a minimum.

"We want you, Kate," Mike said, leaping to his feet and joining Trevor.

"Yeah, we want you." Trent and Travis echoed almost at the same time.

"That's a lot of loving you have there," Bryan commented.

"A person can never have too much." And you shouldn't be afraid of it, Bryan Marlowe, she added silently.

Kate rose and looked at the boys who encircled her. "Now, off with you. You've still got to comb your hair and get your jackets, the lot of you."

They thundered off.

Bryan wiped his lips and rose to his feet. Kate looked in his direction. "May I be excused?" he asked with a hint of sarcasm.

She glanced at his plate. "Now that you've finished, yes."

"I'm surprised you haven't color-coded me."

"I don't need to. You're taller than the rest."

"And older."

"Chronologically."

"I'm not a small, frightened boy, Kate."

"No," she agreed. "You're not small."

He knew what she was alluding to and became annoyed at how transparent he must be. He changed the subject. "Trevor seems very attached to you."

"I know." She ran her hands up and down her arms, looking toward the living room where the boys had gone to collect their things. Then she tuned to face Bryan. "It's not a bad thing," she said, sensing his concern. "He needs to be attached to someone for now. My brother Kevin had an old dog once. It just wandered into the yard one day and became his. Heathcliff, he called it." She smiled fondly as she recalled the memory. "He loved that mangy old thing, but it wasn't meant to live much longer. When Heathcliff died, Kevin was absolutely inconsolable. Withdrew from all of us. No one could even talk to him. Like Trevor when his mother died."

"Kate, I—" There was a warning note in his voice again. He didn't want Jill brought up. He was having more than enough trouble dealing with life since she had come into his.

No, this is too important, Kate thought firmly, refusing to give ground. She went on. "Not to go comparing your late wife with a dog," she clarified, lest he misunderstand her meaning and take offense, "but the grief of losing anything precious to you is immeasurable when you're a little child. Abandoned is abandoned. Anyway, we all scraped together and got enough money to get a puppy from the pound—"

That didn't make any sense to him. Was she making it all up? "Dogs from the pound are free."

She smiled sadly. "It was the license we had to pay for."

He was embarrassed for bringing up her poverty. "Sorry."

Kate waved a hand to dismiss his word. "It took Kevin a while, but eventually he opened up enough to let that puppy in. Once he did that, the rest was easy.''

He knew he should let the matter drop, but for some reason, he couldn't. "Are you our pound puppy?''

"I've been called worse things.''

"By whom?'' He couldn't see anyone saying anything bad to her. She might be momentarily infuriating, but she had a way of taking the edge off any anger directed her way.

"By my brothers and sisters, when I was making them mind their manners.'' She saw Mike running from Travis and decided it was time to referee again. She crossed to the other room without missing a beat. "Well, enough about my family. On to yours. When would be a good time to interview the ladies?'' She gave a warning look to the two boys, and they retreated, picking up their backpacks.

Bryan looked at his watch. So much for missing morning traffic. "Not now.''

"I know that.'' She followed him to the door. "But when?''

"I'll call you from the office,'' he tossed over his shoulder as he hurried to the garage and his car.

Kate stepped out into the front yard. "Mind that you do.''

She definitely acted as if he were one of her charges, he thought as he backed out his car. He saw her waving at him. He waved back. She'd probably make one hell of a snake charmer, he thought with a sudden grin as he drove away.

Bryan kept watching her in his rearview mirror until he turned the corner.

* * *

He hated interviewing people. He and Kate had been at it for two days now, and still they had found no one.

"Thank you, Miss Randolph." Bryan looked over the applicant's head and toward where Kate was sitting. With an almost infinitesimal motion, Kate moved her head from side to side.

Bryan rose and shook the thin woman's hand. "We'll keep you in mind."

He waited until the woman left before turning to Kate. "And what was wrong with her?"

Kate looked surprised at his question. "I thought it was evident. The woman had no sense of humor."

He was growing impatient with the whole process. There were better ways to spend the weekend than asking an odd collection of women how they felt about cleaning up after four small boys. "Kate, I won't be paying her to laugh. I'll be paying her to clean."

She didn't rise to his tone. "You want your sons to be comfortable, don't you?"

Bryan circled her and put his hands on the back of her chair. He lowered his face toward hers. "What does a sense of humor have to do with that?"

"Think," she answered simply. Overhead, the boys were playing some game and running up and down the hall, laughing. It sounded like an army performing maneuvers. Noisy maneuvers.

I am thinking, but it's not of the boys, not when I'm so close to you.

Bryan threw up his hands and walked back to his own chair. "Kate, I'd appreciate it if you didn't treat me as if I were one of your charges."

"I wasn't aware I was doing that, sir."

"And I'm the Prince of Wales."

"You're much better-looking, Mr. Marlowe."

He didn't know whether to laugh, kiss her or surrender. He had a feeling he'd be doing all three
shortly, but perhaps not in that order. For now,
though, he had a housekeeper to find. He waved a
hand at the door. "Who's next, Kate?"

"I have a Mrs. O'Brien waiting in the living
room."

He detected approval in her voice. "Any good?"

Kate shrugged a little too nonchalantly. "She looks
perfect. And she has a twinkle in her eye."

He was going to wind up surrendering to someone
who was a cross between an Irish fairy and a crazy
woman, he thought with a touch of sinking despair.
"Well, then, by all means, let's hire her. Twinkles are
hard to come by."

Kate paused by the door on her way out. "You
know your problem, Mr. Marlowe?"

"I know exactly what my problem is," he said
softly. "My life seems to have been taken over by a
headstrong woman who doesn't listen to a word I
say." What's worse, I don't seem to mind it as much
as I should.

"Oh, I listen, all right. I just use my judgment."

"Oh, I see."

"And your problem is that you're a cynic. You've
forgotten how to laugh."

"More laughter," he muttered.

"No, not enough, I'm afraid," she said quietly as
she left the room.

What was she to do with the man? Kate wondered

as she went toward the den. He needed brightening. At times, she thought she was getting through to him, at other times...well, the battle wasn't over yet.

"Mr. Marlowe, I'd like to introduce Mrs. O'Brien." Kate ushered a woman into the room who was only slightly taller than she was and much, much rounder. At a glance, the gray-haired woman looked as if she had been created to be someone's grandmother. A very capable grandmother.

Kate was right, he thought. The woman looked warm and understanding. And there *was* a twinkle in her eye. It occurred to Bryan that Kate was right about a lot of things. It was hard keeping your guard up against a woman who was never wrong.

Kate exchanged glances with Bryan. He could read her thoughts in her expression. She was gloating.

For some reason, he was determined to find a flaw with Mrs. O'Brien. Kate couldn't *always* be right.

Five minutes into the interview, he knew he had his housekeeper. Her references were a mile long, her warmth and charm abundant. He didn't need to look any further. Kate had been right. Again. He tried to console himself that at least the two-day search was over.

"Mrs. O'Brien, the job is yours. Can you start Monday?"

"I can and I will." The plump woman squeezed his hand warmly when he took hers. "From what Kate tells me, I'm going to love working here."

He looked back at Kate. She had made up her mind about the woman before he had ever seen her. He wasn't used to people making decisions for him. Jill had always left everything up to his judgment when it came to the house, and the housekeepers had all naturally deferred to him. Kate, it seemed, had a mind all her own.

He wasn't altogether sure if he liked that.

But at the moment, his curiosity was aroused. "When did you and Ms. Llewellyn discuss this position?"

"When she called me about it," Mrs. O'Brien answered.

Now he was even more confused. He had thought that that was the agency's function. Was Kate taking over for them, too? Somehow, he wouldn't be surprised. "Why didn't the agency call you?"

"Agency?" Mrs. O'Brien repeated. She looked at Kate, then back at Bryan.

Bryan saw Kate look a little uncertain. Now what? "After yesterday's applicants, I was beginning to despair that perhaps we wouldn't find anyone suitable for quite some time," Kate began, talking rapidly. "Not wanting to waste any more of your time, I put in a call of my own. Mr. Marlowe, I didn't want this affecting your choice—"

Like hell you didn't, he thought, suppressing a wry smile.

"But now that you've chosen her yourself, I'd like to present my Aunt Molly."

"Your aunt," he repeated. He was beginning to feel surrounded. By Kate.

"Molly," Kate prompted.

Now that he looked more carefully, there was a slight resemblance in the smiles. And the eyes. Molly's were the same shade. "Your aunt." He knew he should be angry at her for not telling him, for taking this upon herself, but he wasn't. His reaction worried him.

"That doesn't change anything, does it?" Kate asked. "She's a very hard worker, Mr. Marlowe. I wouldn't have brought her to you if she weren't."

No, he knew she wouldn't. How had he come to know her so well in so short a time? What was there about her that *made* him know these things? But he couldn't let her off the hook so easily.

"Do you have any other relatives around? A gardener, perhaps?"

Molly laughed softly to herself. He was going to like her, too, Bryan decided.

Kate looked at him, perplexed. "Why would I have a gardener?"

"Just wondering if I was going to be besieged by any more members of your family." He turned to the older woman. He took her hand in both of his. There was a comforting feel to her clasp. He might have known. "Welcome to our home, Molly."

Bryan looked at his wristwatch for the third time in eleven minutes. She was late.

He rolled down his shirtsleeves and rebuttoned them. He was being ridiculous. He had never said that she had to report to him every night. It had just become a habit of hers to stop by his den at the end of the day while he was preparing the next day's work. She would sit down and share the day's activities with him.

All right, so her nightly reports had only been going on for three weeks. But he had come to expect them. After all, it was his right as an employer to hear how she was taking care of his sons.

He wadded up the piece of paper he was writing on. Who the hell was he kidding? If that was all he was interested in, he didn't need her to come by each evening with a report. He had eyes. He could see. His sons were thriving, especially Trevor. They were still lively, but not destructively so as they had been. He wasn't under constant pressure to discipline them himself.

He wasn't waiting for her to hear about the day's events. No, he was waiting for her, because he liked having her in this small room with its smell of leather and wood. She brought something special in, a fragrance of...what?

Hope.

Silly word. It had no place in his life. *She* had no place in his life.

And yet, she was here. And he liked it, heaven help him.

He heard her sneeze before she came in. He looked down, pretending to be working and knew that she'd see right through it. She seemed to see right through everything.

Kate sat down in the chair facing his desk. "I'm sorry I'm late, but I had trouble getting the boys to go to sleep, what with the coughing and sneezing. The triplets are down with the flu, and it looks as if Mike is going to be next." Her voice sounded a good deal huskier than normal. She sneezed again.

Bryan leaned over and pulled out a tissue from the box on the side of his desk. He offered it to her. "No, from the sound of it, I'd say you were next."

She smiled gratefully as she took the tissue.

"Trent told me that you stayed up all night with him."

She shrugged off the thanks in his voice. "That's what you do with a sick boy."

That hadn't been what Jill had done. She had left that to the housekeeper, or to him. "Isn't this interfering with your studies?"

That he even cared about how she was managing pleased her greatly.

"I can manage." She sneezed again. She felt her eyes get watery. God, she must look horrible. "I took all the boys to the doctor this afternoon. He said there wasn't anything wrong that a little medicine and rest couldn't cure."

He tucked a strand of wayward hair behind her ear. Compassion mixed with desire stirred within him. "You look as if you need some rest yourself."

She gave him a weak smile. She was beginning to feel pretty miserable at that. "Haven't you heard? I'm indestructible. At least your sons think that."

"Wonder who gave them that idea."

"Haven't the foggiest."

He rose from his desk and moved behind her. "You look terrible."

"Careful, Mr. Marlowe, you'll be turning my head with your flattery." Her eyes were still watery. She used the tissue to wipe away the tears that had formed. She turned to get a better look at him. The movement made her wince.

"What's the matter?"

"My shoulder." She rubbed it as she said the words. "I think that's where the cold is spreading."

Without thinking, Bryan put his hands on her shoulder and began to knead very slowly. "Better?"

"Better than better. Heaven." She sighed and closed her eyes.

He saw the dark lashes sweep her cheek. Heard her sigh. Instinct took over where common sense would have declared a halt.

He turned the swivel chair around and bent over to kiss her. The kiss grew in intensity, and he wasn't certain if he lifted her from the chair to her feet or if she moved up to meet him. Either way, the kiss caught fire.

Kate drew back to catch her breath. "You'll catch my germs," she warned, but she didn't want him to stop. The misery of the flu temporarily faded. Nothing existed except his wonderful mouth and the fiery effect it had on her. She drew herself up on her toes. He was so tall, he made her head spin. Or was that the cold? Or something else entirely? She didn't know, she didn't care. All she cared about was right here in her arms.

I love you, Bryan Marlowe. And I'm going to find a way to make your pain go away.

His hands went beneath her sweater, encircling her small waist even while his mind told him to stop. She felt so soft, so delicate. Later he'd pay for it and with more than a cold, he knew. But for now, he needed to have her here, to feel her against him, to drink from the sweet well that she offered him.

He pressed her against him, his desire heating as his body did the same.

Over and over again, his mouth slanted over hers, taking, giving, wanting her more than he had ever thought he could want a woman. Was it just deprivation, or could it possibly be—?

The single unformed word within his mind frightened the hell out of him.

wouldn't be could work a miracle. What if just once

to — only it possible to —

"He stuffs himself work with out ever feel" To he

find the fact of his mind.

Chapter Eight

He kissed her with an intensity born of abstinence and framed in a love he couldn't deny. He wanted to absorb her, to absorb the radiance she seemed to possess. Just for now, he'd let himself believe it was real. Holding her face in his hands, he kissed her cheeks, her lips, her eyes. He ached for her so badly. For one moment, his control slipped away. The exhilarating rush of freedom it brought was almost too much to bear.

But a multitude of established emotions continued to war within him, retrenching, regaining position. With effort, Bryan pulled himself away. He could have so easily gotten lost in the softness he found here, within the sweetness Kate had to offer. But he wouldn't let himself. Fall in love with one person, watch someone else evolve. It had happened to him once, it could happen again. No, he couldn't go through that again, *wouldn't* go through that.

He called himself a coward. But right now it took more courage not to give in to the needs that cried out for satisfaction within him.

"I've no business kissing you."

She saw the change in his eyes. There was agony there now, just under the surface. Why? What was he so afraid of? "Perhaps. But you do go about business very, very well, Mr. Marlowe." Her voice was low, husky with emotion she sensed he couldn't deal with.

He resisted the desire to hold her to him again. "I'm sorry."

His stiff apology hurt, but she tried not to show it. "You always seem to be making apologies where none are necessary." She drew a breath and tried to hold her words back. She knew from his expression that it would do no good to try to discuss things now. But running away wasn't her way. "What you should be sorry about is shutting yourself off from feelings."

Bryan stepped back from her. His voice was dangerously quiet. "Am I getting the benefit of your education, Ms. Llewellyn?"

Damn you, don't clam up on me. "You're getting the benefit of another human being caring. A shoulder to cry on."

It would be so easy to care for her. He wanted to so very badly. But he couldn't. It wouldn't be fair to either of them. "I don't cry."

"A pity."

Her response angered him. He didn't need her pity. He didn't need her looking into his soul this way. "Psychology major or not, you don't know what you're talking about."

What an infuriatingly exasperating man! "Then tell

me what it is I don't understand. I'm willing to listen.''

He had to get away from her, from those eyes that did things to him. He looked pointedly at his watch. "It's late."

She touched his arm and forced him to look at her. He read so much in her eyes, none of which he wanted to see. "But it's not too late."

"Good night, Kate. Take care of your cold."

Kate moved toward the door. The dismissal stung. She wondered if it came from his heart, or from whatever devil it was he lived with. Maybe she should have her head examined for caring so much. But she did care, there was no getting around it. "And you'd better take care of what ails you before it does you in," she said as she left.

He didn't bother looking up. "Right."

The encounter kept Bryan awake that night. Her face was there every time he closed his eyes. He couldn't rid himself of it, nor of his desire for her. Kate was too good to be true. But that was the way he had once felt about Jill, about the life they were going to share together. Because he wanted to, needed to, he had perceived in her his own desires, his own dreams. But she had obviously had different needs. And living with his expectations had ultimately destroyed her.

Well, he thought, turning restlessly in bed, it wasn't going to happen again. Better to go without expectations than to feel disappointed and guilty. He couldn't handle it again. He made up his mind.

Yet an elusive inner voice refused to be silenced. This wasn't him. This was the coward's way out.

She's the best thing that ever happened to you, and you know it.

No, he didn't know it, he thought fiercely. He didn't know anything. Not when it came to women. He was safer sticking to the law and to the care and nurturing of his sons.

He sneezed just before he went to sleep. It occurred to him that he had most probably caught her cold. Served him right for his moment of weakness.

She didn't have time for this.

Kate struggled out of bed, feeling as if an invisible hand was pushing down heavily on her chest. She felt absolutely awful. She had gotten very little sleep this past week. The triplets were over their flu attack, and it seemed to have bypassed Mike, despite early signs to the contrary. But she had come down with a triple whammy.

"You look good enough to haunt houses," she said to the reflection she saw in her bathroom mirror.

She'd skip classes today, she decided. Just ferry the boys to school and pick them up at two. If she lived that long.

Her deep, hacking cough preceded her down the stairs.

"That sounds like a bear," Mike said. The boys looked a little uncertainly at their father.

"More like a stubborn woman who won't stay in bed," Bryan answered.

"I'd wager you don't run into that problem very

much,'' Molly observed drily as she put down a platter of bacon in the center of the table.

"Only with your niece." He saw the woman's eyebrows rise. "I meant that in the best way possible," he added quickly.

The smile Molly wore was one that often graced Kate's lips. "I wonder." She turned back to her work.

The whole family was nuts, Bryan decided.

He looked up as Kate entered the room. She was dressed in jeans and a sweater and looked appallingly miserable. He had an uncontrollable urge to pick her up and carry her to bed. More impulsive thoughts. Kate seemed to bring them out in him.

Bryan rose and towered over her. "You're going back to bed."

Kate shuffled over to the refrigerator. When had it moved so far from the table? She indicated the boys. "After." She pulled out a container of orange juice and poured herself a glass. The juice hurt her throat.

"Now."

Kate put down the glass and looked at Bryan. "Is that an order?"

"Yes."

She shook her head, immediately regretting it. The room swam. "Sorry, I never follow orders."

"Well, then," Bryan grinned, making a sudden decision to go with impulse, "we'll just have to make you, won't we boys?"

She felt too weak to struggle against what she suspected would follow. The boys surrounded her, and then Bryan cut through the crowd and picked her up bodily.

She hated to admit it, but being off her feet felt

wonderful. She struggled not to show her relief and found she had no strength with which to fake a protest. She did, however, manage to raise an eyebrow. Just one. "And just what is it you have in mind, Mr. Marlowe?"

"We won't go into that—" Kate wondered if that was a momentary wicked gleam in his eye or if she were hallucinating "—but I am putting you to bed for your own good."

"The boys—" she protested, pointing to the gathering. They faded away, and she realized that Bryan was walking toward the stairs.

"I can certainly take them to school," Molly called from the kitchen.

"Well, if you think it's all right..." Kate's voice trailed off as she settled back in Bryan's arms. Nice. Very, very nice. Even with her head throbbing and growing to three times its normal size, this was nice.

"I think it's all right," Bryan affirmed. "I told you to take care of that cold."

"It's the flu."

He reached the top of the stairs. "You do like to argue, don't you?"

"One of my bad habits."

She was becoming a habit with him, he thought. "Like nagging?"

"I don't nag," she pretended to sniff. "I remind."

"Several times."

"If need be."

Bryan pushed open the door to her bedroom with his shoulder, then crossed over to her bed. "Now, let's get you into bed."

"Why, Mr. Marlowe," she said weakly, her hand to her breast, "this is so sudden."

She was hot, obviously running a fever, yet he could have taken her there and then if the house hadn't been filled with small people who could barge in unannounced.

Oh Kate, Kate, what have you done to me? You're taking me to places I swore I'd never go to again.

"Don't tempt me, Kate."

"Do I?" She fought to keep her eyes opened. "Do I tempt you?"

He placed her on the bed, moving aside the comforter. "More than you'll ever know," he said very softly.

But she heard. "Someday," she said softly, settling back, "you'll have to show me." She was asleep one second after she uttered the last word.

"That's just what I'm afraid of doing, Kate." He covered her with the comforter, then quietly slipped out and closed the door.

"You're taking too much upon yourself, girl." Molly looked sternly over the tops of her bifocals at her niece as she slowly trimmed the excess dough from the cherry pie she was preparing. It was several days later, and Kate swore she was back up to par. She had insisted on taking the boys to school and then had attended her two classes for the day.

"That's why Mr. Marlowe hired you, to take some of the load off my shoulders, remember?" Kate patted her aunt's soft, wrinkled cheek.

"You know what I'm saying. I'm talking about your studies, the boys. Him."

Kate put her hands on her hips in mock indignation. Her voice took on an Irish brogue. She sounded a great deal, she thought, like her mother had. "And when was it that I couldn't handle a few small boys and me studies, I'll be wantin' to know? Spent most of my childhood that way, I did." She watched her aunt open her mouth, and she knew what was coming. She raced in to head off the woman's words. "As for 'him,' I'm afraid 'himself' won't let me do anything at all for his situation."

Molly put the small knife down on the counter. It clattered against the blue tile. She took no notice. Instead, she leveled a gaze at Kate. "Katie, it's not your place—"

Kate pretended to be busy cleaning up in order to avoid her aunt's astute look. "It's every human being's place to do something when they see another human being hurting the way he is." Kate gave up the ruse and turned to look at her aunt. "He never goes out, never socializes. All he does is work."

"Humph. Like someone else I might mention." Molly wiped her hands on her flour-dotted apron.

Kate shook her head and laughed. "This isn't work. I love it." Kate opened the oven for her aunt.

Molly slipped the pie in, then slowly closed the door. "Well, maybe so does he."

"He's not a workaholic by choice. I can tell."

"Moira never told me that you were into readin' minds."

"Mother forgot to tell you that, did she?" Kate clasped her arms around the older woman's shoulders and gave her a warm hug. Flour dusted her sweater. "I'm into reading hearts, Aunt Molly."

Molly brushed the white traces from her niece's sweater. "That you are. But I can't help worrying."

"I thank you for caring. Now mind you watch that pie. I'm bringing four hungry boys home in thirty minutes, and I'll wager that that pie isn't going to see the dinner table."

Kate grabbed her purse and sailed out the door.

When she pulled the car up to the school yard, the boys were already in the play area, waiting for her. When they saw the car, they raced over. Kate hit the proper button on the control panel beneath her left hand, and the doors unlocked.

"We got out early," Trent and Travis chorused together. Mike and Trevor both tried to get into the front seat of the car in an attempt to sit next to Kate.

"Hey, get back, runt," Mike threatened.

"Take that back!" Trevor cried.

"Runt, runt, runt."

"Boys!" Kate's voice rose above the heated argument. She looked pointedly at Mike. "You know whose turn it is. Today is red day, and red is—" She paused, waiting.

"Trevor," Mike mumbled. He climbed back out. As he did, he glared at his brother.

"And I'd like to hear an apology, please."

"I'm sorry you're a runt," Mike muttered to his brother.

"Michael."

He knew he was in trouble, even though her voice was soft and low. She never used his full name unless he had grossly erred.

Mike looked at Trevor sheepishly. "I didn't mean to call you a runt."

"That's better." She smiled at Mike, and he immediately brightened. "We all say things we don't mean when we're angry."

"Not you, Katie," Trevor cried loyally.

"Oh, yes, me. I'm not a saint." Kate patted the seat next to her. "Hop on here, Trevor."

The boy sat down, grinning with triumph.

"All right, you know the rules. You have to tell me what you did today."

She had started the system in part to rule out the fights about who sat where. This way, they proceeded in a rotating fashion, each boy getting a turn to sit next to her, as well as next to the window. It was also a discreet way to encourage Trevor to take part in things. He tended to be drowned out by his brothers and seemed not to want to make the effort to assert himself.

Beneath his brothers' envious eyes, Trevor made himself comfortable in the seat of honor next to Kate and slowly, with only a minimum of prodding on her part, told her what he had done in kindergarten that day.

Kate felt a kind of warmth wind through her as she drove home. At least she could help some of the Marlowe men, if not all of them.

"I've been meaning to talk to you," Kate said as she watched the boys gather around Bryan, vying for his attention.

Bryan had just walked in through the door. He had become used to her descending upon him, on the heels of his sons. Hell, if he were honest with himself, he looked forward to it. How had things happened so fast, he wondered. How did things get away from him so completely?

"Okay, guys, wrestling match postponed until Kate has her say." He looked at her over the heads of two of his sons. "Yes?"

"I think it might be time to enroll the boys in some kind of sport."

Bryan put his attaché case on the hall table and slipped his jacket off. Trevor grabbed it from him. Instead of playing with it, pretending to be his father, he hurried off to the closet, holding it aloft in order not to get it dirty.

That was a new one, Bryan thought. They were learning to be neat. He blessed Kate and the progress she had made. "Anything but karate."

"Hey, yeah!" Travis's eyes took on a glow as he assumed a standard stance. He delivered a karate chop to Trent, who promptly punched him.

Very calmly Kate came between the two. She never stopped talking to Bryan. "I was thinking along the lines of baseball, actually. That's enough of a demonstration," she told the boys.

To Bryan's amazement, the two separated. The woman had a gift, she truly did.

For more things than one, he thought.

A delicious aroma floated in from the kitchen. He walked in that direction as he thought over Kate's suggestion. "Baseball?" The boys trailed behind. He nodded a greeting at Molly, who was placing dinner on the table.

Under Kate's watchful eye, the boys all took their

proper seats. "It would teach them discipline and the meaning of teamwork."

It seemed to him that she had a pretty good handle on discipline already. "I'm for that." He sat down.

"Then it's all right?"

He spread his hands wide. "I have no objections. And even if I did, I have a feeling you'd find a way to overrule them."

Kate sat down, facing him from the other end of the table. The way a wife would, he caught himself thinking.

"Why, Mr. Marlowe, I'd never go against your wishes."

He saw the laughter in her eyes. "But you'd work at it until my wishes coincided with yours."

"That's democracy, isn't it?" Her full lips rose in a smile.

That's sorcery, he wanted to say, but didn't.

The next day she found a team willing to take the boys. Bryan marveled at how fast she worked, then laughed at his own surprise. Hadn't she managed to work her way into his subconscious at lightning speed?

That was only, he reminded himself, because he had been alone for so long. It was only natural for a man's desires to be stirred up by an attractive woman.

He knew he was lying.

He had had contact with enough attractive women to know that it was more than that. Attractive women merely left him cold. For the last two years, all women had. Kate Llewellyn had that something extra that infiltrated his mind and body and gave him no peace. At times he was sorry he had hired her, but he knew he was being selfish. Look what she had done for the boys. She was more of a mother than a caretaker. She interested herself in the boys' well-being, not just in their care and feeding.

He blessed the whimsy of fate that had sent her his way.

If only fate hadn't made her so damn desirable, he thought.

The intercom on his desk buzzed, interrupting his thoughts. He pressed the button.

"Ms. Llewellyn on line three, Mr. Marlowe."

Bryan jerked up the receiver. Kate never called him at work. He heard an unfamiliar din in the background. "What's wrong?"

"Nothing yet, but it will be if you don't leave the office right now."

"Kate, what are you talking about?"

"The game, Mr. Marlowe," Kate said patiently. "You're supposed to be here right now, attending the boys' first game."

Damn. The Richter case had blocked everything else from his mind. "I completely forgot."

"I had a feeling."

There was what sounded like a roar in the background. "What's that noise behind you?"

She put her finger in her ear in order to hear him better. "I'm calling from a phone across the street from the playing field. That's traffic and anxious boys you hear." She paused. "Well?"

It occurred to him that half the time she spoke in strange riddles that she expected him to have the answers to. "Well, what?"

"Why aren't you hanging up and coming?"

He looked at his work. Sons were more important. She always helped him keep sight of that. He chided himself for forgetting. Most of the games were scheduled on weekends, but this was the first one of the season. Workday or not, he wanted to be there. He closed the folder on his desk. "Yes, Mother."

"Your mother is a lovely lady who lives on Holland Drive. I'm just Kate Llewellyn—"

"Oh no, there is no 'just' in front of your name, Kate. There is no such thing as 'just' a hurricane. I'm leaving right now."

"Good."

She smiled to herself as she hung up. His backhanded compliment played itself over again in her mind. "I'll get you to come around yet, Bryan Marlowe. See if I don't," she whispered as she turned around.

"Dad's not here, Kate," Mike pointed out.

"Just talking to myself, Mike."

He looked at her strangely, not understanding.

The others looked at her impatiently. "Is he going to come, Kate?" Trent asked. "Is he?"

She took his hand and Trevor's and began to cross the street, trusting Mike to look out for his other brother. "He wouldn't miss it for the world." She glanced to her right to make sure that Mike was doing what was expected of him. He was.

"But you had to call him to remind him to come," Travis said, pouting.

They crossed to the edge of the playing field. A semicircle of bleachers stood to the right. Kate prudently let go of the boys' hands. Boys had to appear independent to their peers. "That's because he left his watch home today and forgot what time it was."

Her excuse satisfied them and soothed potential hurt feelings.

It was the bottom of the sixth. Kate kept one eye on the game and one out for Bryan. It made for a headache. But she finally saw him to the left of the field. He was the only one there in a three-piece suit. But he was there.

She waved frantically until he saw her.

Bryan waved back, relieved to have found her in this sea of cheering people. He worked his way through the rows of parents until he reached her. Suddenly overcome with weariness, he sank down in the space she was saving for him. It wasn't very large, and he found his thigh pressed up against hers. It took effort not to think about that.

"Sorry I'm late. There was an overturned truck on the freeway." He looked at the field, trying to pick out his sons. The players all looked alike from this vantage point. "How are we doing?"

"How are you at sympathy?"

He looked back at her. "That bad?"

She gave him what passed for a brave smile. "Do you remember the Mets when they first started out?"

"That bad." He sighed, running his hand through his hair. The wind kept tangling it. "Maybe this wasn't such a good idea."

"They have to know how to lose as well as win," Kate pointed out.

He looked at the scoreboard. There was no number next to the home team. "But fifteen to zero?"

"They'll get better."

"They'll have to. The only way they'd get worse is if they owed a run to the other team."

Kate laughed. Carelessly she brushed aside the hair that fell in her eyes. The wind was gusting now, teasing strands of hair about her face.

"You're right," she said.

"About what?"

"You do have a sense of humor in there somewhere."

He banked down his thoughts of her and turned his attention to his sons. "I think we're going to need it once this game is over."

"Boy, what a disaster," Mike muttered. He seemed embarrassed as he trudged over to his father. His brothers followed close behind him, one more forlorn than the other.

Bryan was searching for something encouraging to say. He looked to Kate for help and realized how dependent on her he was becoming.

She didn't fail him. "It's not a disaster if you learned something from it." She put her arm around Mike.

"Yeah," Trent complained loudly. "Not to play baseball." He threw down his cap.

Wordlessly Kate stooped down and picked it up. Carefully she dusted the cap off. "That's not what I meant, Trent. Losing builds character."

"I don't want character," he pouted. "I wanna win."

She held the cap out to him. "Then you'll practice harder, won't you?" she encouraged.

The boy nodded and took the cap back.

"How about you, Trevor?" she asked.

"If you want me to." His response was eager.

She knew he liked to please her, but that was not what she wanted from him. "No, it's what you want that counts."

"I wanna be good," he answered.

"Then practice."

It was a complete shutout, Bryan thought. The boys now all related to her far better than they did to him. They turned to her with their hurt, and she was the go-between, the one who smoothed things outs. Like a good mother, he thought. Again the thought of having her permanently in his life raised itself. The idea of marriage whispered its presence in his ear. What if he took the chance? She seemed to be perfect.

Seemed. That was just the trouble. Could he risk everything on appearance, on his own judgment? On his own desires? His desires and needs had colored things once. This time, if he were wrong, if things didn't work out, the boys would be old enough to be really hurt. They were attached to Kate. Why mess things up? It was best if he just left things the way they were. Then everyone would be happy.

Or would they?

He continued to watch Kate quietly, his expression giving no hint of what was on his mind.

Kate looked at the small gathering before her. "Personally I think you did terrific for your first time. Even the best baseball players have bad days and bad starts." She rattled off a few statistics that raised the boys' spirits and made Bryan wonder if there was any information that she didn't have at her disposal.

Travis echoed his sentiments. "Gosh, Kate, you know everything."

"No, but I'm working on it." She put her hands around two of the boys' shoulders. "What say we go out for some pizza and celebrate your entry into the world of baseball?"

The boys all cheered their approval.

Kate turned and looked at Bryan. "Mr. Marlowe?"

"What?" he asked innocently. "Me? I thought I was only here for the ride."

She tucked her arm through his. "No, not just for the ride." She looked up at his face brightly. "Also to pay the check."

He laughed in spite of himself. She made him feel good. "Anyone ever tell you you have a silver tongue?"

"They've hinted at it." The laughter in her eyes dissipated a little as they held his. He saw a softened look, a look that touched something within him. He found himself wanting her again, here, in this improbable place.

But then the look was gone, and she turned back to the boys. "You're all going to be wonderful players," she promised them as she ushered all four into the station wagon. "I can just feel it."

She slammed the door and came around to the driver's side. Bryan was standing there, waiting.

"Doesn't your plane ever land, Kate?"

"Why should it land? Life is too glorious and too brief to spend it in sadness." And I'm going to teach you that, or die trying, she vowed silently.

He shrugged. "If you say so."

"I say so."

For one brief moment, he wondered what life would be like with Kate if he had the courage to ask her to be his wife.

Probably not what you think, he told himself, pushing the thought away.

"I'll meet you there," he said, walking over to the car he had driven.

"You bet you will," she called after him.

He had the strangest feeling that they were not talking about the pizza parlor.

Chapter Nine

He had done it in a moment of weakness, and now he was paying for it.

As he hurriedly got dressed, Bryan began to wonder if insanity was catching. If it was, he knew he had caught it from Kate. Why else would he have suggested their going out for dinner to celebrate her being with the family for a month?

Insanity, pure and simple.

No, he reconsidered, there was nothing simple about it. And, if his thoughts were examined, he wouldn't get any points for purity, either.

Bryan fought with the knot in his tie. The knot was winning.

The familiar sounds of an argument in progress down the hall grew closer. Suddenly his domain was invaded by Mike and Travis.

"Dad'll say I'm right," Mike insisted.

"Will not. I am!" Travis cried.

They turned toward their father and then stared, the argument forgotten.

"That bad?" Bryan asked.

Mike's brows drew together as he examined his father. Bryan normally changed into jeans and a sweatshirt after he came home, not another suit. "How come you look like that?" Mike wanted to know.

"I'm going out to dinner."

The shower he had just taken was supposed to have refreshed him. It had. For approximately three minutes. And then the tenseness that had been plaguing him ever since he had made the date for dinner returned. Bryan tried to ignore it.

"By yourself?" Mike asked suspiciously.

"No."

"With who?" the boys asked together.

Bryan reached for his comb and tried to sound as nonchalant as possible. "Kate." As he looked in the mirror, he saw Mike and Travis exchange puzzled glances behind him.

Mike vaulted onto his father's bed and rested his chin on his hands. "Can't you eat with her here?" he wanted to know.

"It's not quite the same thing." But it probably would be a good deal wiser. He knew that he was about to make a step from which there would be no turning back, yet he still persisted in doing it. If that wasn't insanity, what was?

The meaning behind his words was lost on Travis. "Can we come, too?"

"No, you wouldn't like it. It's one of those restaurants that doesn't serve hamburgers or pizza."

Travis shook his head knowingly. "She won't like it, either."

"I'll chance it." Mike was studying him very intently, his face propped up on his knuckles. Bryan turned around to face him. "Something wrong?"

"You gonna marry her?"

"What!"

Mike scrambled up and swung his legs over the side of the bed. "Well, she's living here with us and you're living here, so I thought that maybe…" He let the rest of the sentence trail off as he cocked his head and looked at his father, waiting.

Bryan scrutinized his tie. The knot was lopsided. Why was he all thumbs tonight? "Mike, other women have lived here before Kate. You've never asked that question about them."

"Yeah," Travis chimed in, "but they were all old people. Even older than you."

This was as good as it got, he decided, giving up on the tie. "Thanks."

"Kate's young and pretty and nice," Travis continued, "Don't you like her?"

Just what he needed, midget matchmakers working against him. "Yes, I like her."

Mike closed in on his other side. "So why don't you marry her?"

"It's a little more complicated than that, Mike."

"Why?" Mike persisted. Travis silently echoed the question with his puzzled expression.

"I don't know Mike, it just is."

Mike shrugged. "Don't seem that complicated to me. Well, if you don't want her, can I marry her?"

Bryan laughed. "I think you have to be taller. Go drink your milk."

Mike disappeared with a very determined look on his face. Travis was right behind him.

Bryan wished he possessed half of his son's simple, direct outlook on things. He was nervous about tonight, really nervous, even though he tried to rationalize the feeling away. He realized that he had faced hung juries with more confidence. He felt as if he were about to make a grave mistake, yet there was no graceful way to back out now, and he knew that part of him didn't want to back out. Part of him, albeit a very small part, still believed in happy endings. That was the part that was driving him to do this. Kate had done that to him. She had made him remember what it had been like once, for him.

He closed his eyes and suddenly saw Jill, Jill fading before his eyes like a flower taken out of water. She had been young and vital once, too. And the world had seemed full of promise for them. He opened his eyes. No, things weren't simple, not by a long shot. Mike would learn that all too soon.

Kate appeared in the doorway, and visions of Jill disappeared. Visions of everything disappeared. Kate was wearing a strapless blue dress that matched her eyes, accented her waist and wreaked havoc on his libido.

She crossed her arms before her and leaned against the doorjamb. "Mike tells me that you don't want me and that he'll be marrying me."

"Oh, God," Bryan groaned. He shrugged into his jacket. "Look, Kate—"

There was humor in her eyes. She smoothed down

his upturned collar. "What I want to know is, will you be paying for the wedding, or is this going to come out of Mike's allowance?"

He took hold of her hands and drew them away from his chest. It was almost as if the heat from her fingertips had seared right through the material and touched him. She was always touching him in ways he had not thought possible. "We'll discuss it over dinner."

"Dinner with my father-in-law-to-be." Kate slipped her arm through his as they headed toward the stairs. "This should be an interesting evening."

"Funny, I had the same thought." He stopped as they passed her room.

Kate turned to look at him. "What's the matter?"

"Your shoulders."

"What about them?"

"They're bare."

She glanced at either side. "Yes, they are."

"Do you think that's wise?"

She caught a strange look in his eyes. Afraid of me. He's afraid of me for some reason, she thought suddenly, then dismissed the thought as being utterly absurd. No one was afraid of her. "For whom?"

Her shoulders were silky-soft and demanded caressing. For me, he thought.

"For you," he said aloud. "You're just getting over the flu."

"You know, you are a very thoughtful person, even though you pretend not to be," Kate said as she ducked into her room. She returned with a lacy white shawl which she handed to him, and then she turned her back.

He slipped it around her shoulders. His fingers lingered there a moment too long, then he withdrew them almost as if he were suddenly conscious of what he was doing.

"Better?" she asked.

Not hardly, he thought. "Better," he muttered as they went down the stairs.

"Then why are you frowning?"

"I'm not frowning."

"Mr. Marlowe." She stopped at the landing and looked him squarely in the eye. "I'm a psychology major. I know a frown when I see one."

"I'll work on it."

She winked. "See that you do."

"Hey, guys, Katie's wearing a dress!" Trent cried, alerting the others. They all came in a rush and circled her.

"Yes," she said with a smile, holding out the full skirt, "on occasion I do wear a dress." She turned around slowly. "Do you like it?"

"You bet!"

"Super."

"You're real pretty," Trevor murmured.

She did a little curtsy. "It's nice to be appreciated, gentlemen."

"How's it stay up?" Mike wanted to know.

"No, Mike—" Bryan began.

"Super Glue," Kate answered deftly.

She saw Bryan suppressing a laugh. The evening's off to a good start, she thought. From the left, Kate saw her aunt entering the room. "Now see that you mind Molly, boys. She's going to give me a complete report when I come back."

"We'll be good, Kate," Travis promised solemnly. The others nodded as they followed them to the door.

"See you later, boys, Molly," Bryan nodded to the older woman. Then he took hold of Kate's arm and ushered her out the door. "I think we'd better make a run for it before anything happens." They made their way to the car in the driveway.

She stood back as he opened the door of the Mercedes. "You're the boss."

Bryan rounded the front of the car and got in on the driver's side. "I sometimes have doubts about that."

She settled back in the car. "Haven't I followed your instructions to the letter?"

"And then some."

"Meaning?"

He glanced at her as they drove down the avenue. "That I believe I got decidedly much more than I bargained for."

Kate knew he wasn't referring to the way she handled his sons. Maybe tonight, veils will finally be lifted. She fervently hoped so. "Is that bad?"

"In a way."

"What way?"

He laughed shortly. "Don't you ever get tired of asking questions?"

"No."

"Well, at least you're honest. I suppose your insatiable thirst for knowledge gives you a lot in common with the crew. They're always asking questions."

"It's how they learn things."

"And what is it that you're trying to learn?" Stupid

question Marlowe. You've left yourself wide open. If you were in court, they would have roasted you.

Yet somehow, he was his own devil's advocate. If he weren't, he wouldn't be here with her now.

"About you."

Her voice was low. It played like a soft, sultry melody on his skin. "I think you know all you need to know, Kate."

She turned her face forward, content to drop the subject for now. "Not by a long shot, Mr. Marlowe, not by a long shot."

He didn't like being addressed so formally, even though it was the wisest way to leave things. "I suppose, for the evening, you should call me Bryan."

"For the evening, then." She nodded her approval. "It would make things a wee bit more comfortable."

I don't know about that, Bryan thought as he turned the car toward Wilshire Boulevard.

His feeling didn't change when they arrived at the restaurant he had chosen. The very intimacy of the place put him on his guard. He had forgotten about the decor when he had made the reservations. The restaurant was dark and romantic and all the things he didn't need to urge him on. Something unconscious and defiant within him was working against him.

And she was working against him as well, just by being near him. It was so easy to get lost in her laughter, in the way she had of saying things, in her lighthearted way of looking at life. It was so easy to forget that he never wanted to become involved with a woman again.

And so, he did.

"Do you dance, Bryan?" she asked as the waiter swept away their plates.

"Yes." He hadn't been dancing in a very long while, not since that trip, he remembered suddenly.

She saw a strange look enter his eyes, and this time, Kate was determined to out-maneuver it before it made him retreat from her. She leaned forward and whispered. "Prove it."

Her breath tickled his ear. The muscles of his stomach tightened. "I beg your pardon?"

"Why? You haven't stepped on my feet yet."

"I don't step on feet."

"Good, that'll make it that much more enjoyable." She put out her hand to him, and he had no choice but to take it.

Actually he did have a choice, he just didn't want to take it, not right now. Later, he'd chastise himself for this, for the whole evening; but for the moment, he'd enjoy this strange Irish fairy who had slipped into his life so effortlessly.

They moved out onto the small dance floor. There were several other couples there, all oblivious to one another, all in worlds of their own.

What would it be like, Bryan wondered, to be that wrapped up in someone else again?

He looked down at Kate, who waited patiently for him to make the first move. "What, aren't you going to lead?"

"No, I thought I'd let you do that."

He took her hand in his. "Thank you."

"You're welcome."

She rested her head against his chest as he slipped

his arm around her waist. He breathed in the fragrance of her hair. Some light, airy thing. Like her. Intoxicating. Also like her. She fit against him so well, as if they had been doing this for a long, long time.

Careful, Bryan.

He ignored his own warning. Bryan leaned his cheek against the soft curtain of her hair. "Tell me, are there any witches in your family, Kate?"

She raised her head to look at him. She tried to read his expression, and couldn't. "None that I know of. Why?"

"I don't know. You seemed to have bewitched the boys." And me as well.

She laid her cheek against his chest again, hiding her smile. "That's called being nice."

"It's more than that."

There was something very pregnant in his words. "Is it, now?" She looked up again. The familiar smile lifted the corners of her mouth and drifted into her eyes. "Tell me about it."

"It's like having a spell cast over them. Over—"

"Yes?"

The music stopped, and he was saved by the silence, he thought. He had almost put his foot into it. "The song's over."

Kate made no move to return to her table. "I suppose that means we'll have to sit down."

"Something like that."

She sighed. "I rather liked it here." Reluctantly she let her hand drop from his.

Odd how he could miss her lightest touch, he thought. He put his hand on the small of her back and escorted her to their table.

He held out her chair for her. "You always speak your mind, don't you?"

"It makes for less misunderstandings that way, don't you think?"

He sat down opposite her, picking up his napkin. "I'm a lawyer, Kate. I know the value of words."

"Oh, is that why you've been hoarding them?"

"Around you, it's hard to get a word in edgewise."

"I don't talk that much."

"Oh yes you do."

She shrugged good-naturedly. He couldn't get his eyes off her bare shoulders. "I just don't like silence. You know, for a lawyer, you *are* awfully close mouthed."

"I prefer to listen."

"I prefer to share." She looked alert as music filtered into the room once again. "Ah, they're playing our song again."

"Our song?"

"Yes." Kate rose and took his hand. She pulled him toward the floor. He didn't go reluctantly. "Music," she clarified.

He laughed, truly laughed, and took her into his arms. He was amazed at how easily this could become a habit, holding her to him like this. For a moment, all his objections, all his carefully thought-out reasons floated out of reach. For now, he was content to sway to some timeless piece that the quartet was playing. He realized that he wouldn't have cared if they were playing a march by John Philip Sousa, just as long as it gave him an excuse to hold her like this and pretend that he wasn't who he was and that reality wasn't some harsh thing that reared its head in the wee hours of the morning, after the mists had faded from his eyes.

He looked down into her upturned face. There was nothing in the world he wanted more than to kiss her. He bent his head and brushed her lips ever so gently with his own. Even that slight contact was electric.

Kate held her breath, wanting to go with it, knowing that she couldn't, not here at least.

There was no getting around it, Kate thought. She was falling in love with him. It had started out so innocently. She had just wanted to alleviate whatever hurt troubled him. She still hadn't done that, but somewhere along the line during her mission of mercy, she had gotten entangled and lost her heart five times over. To the motherless boys who responded to the love she had to offer and to Bryan who seemed afraid of doing that very thing. Where it would all lead, she had no idea. For the first time in her life, Kate was at a loss as to what the future would hold. She who had always been so sure of her goals.

Well, she thought with a smile as they arrived at the front door several hours later, Mike had promised to marry her. There was always that to fall back on.

Bryan glanced at his watch as he took out his key. "It's past midnight. I would have thought you'd have worn out your smile by now."

"It's rechargeable. I thought you knew. Besides—" she hugged herself as she leaned against the door and sighed "—I've had a wonderful evening with a very interesting man. Why shouldn't I be smiling?"

What had he allowed to happen, he thought with a

sense of panic taking over. He didn't want things to go any further between them. And yet...

There was no "yet" about it. He had to do the right thing. He had to stop it before they both got hurt.

"Kate, um, I don't want you to misunderstand." He was aware of her watching him as he fumbled for words. It occurred to him that he never fumbled for words with anyone else. Ever. "I'm very satisfied with what you've done. You've brought order into a world of chaos, and I wanted to show you my appreciation." She saw right through him, and he knew it.

It was more than that and you know it, but we'll play your game a while longer. "Sort of like a gold watch twenty-five years ahead of its time?"

"You're mocking me."

"I never mock, Bryan."

She looked at the front door. Her shawl slipped from her shoulders. Moonlight made them golden. Soft. Inviting. God, how he wanted her.

"Or should I say Mr. Marlowe?" There was a mischievous gleam in her eye.

He gave up trying to be noble. "You shouldn't say anything," he answered as he took her into his arms.

"Whatever you say, Mr. Marlowe," she murmured just before his lips reached hers.

He wanted to consume her, loving and hating her for what she was doing to him, for what she was making him want. He prided himself on his control, and every time he was with her, it slipped further away.

Bryan filled his hands with her hair, wanting to touch her all over, wanting to melt the Super Glue she had told Mike she had used. Her breasts, so tantalizing, pressed against him, making his head swirl with desire, with needs that cried out for fulfillment.

Needs he knew could never be fulfilled.

This was the true man, Kate thought. This was the man she was waiting for. The one who could love. For there was love behind this passionate kiss, she could feel it, taste it. It drugged her, yet made her lucid at the same time. All the questions she had were answered here.

He had to stop, stop now before it got out of hand. If he didn't stop, he'd carry her to his bed and make love to her. With reluctance so startlingly heavy that it took an effort to move, Bryan raised his head. "It's late," he breathed against her face.

"I know," she sighed, her eyes not leaving his. "The coach has turned into a pumpkin, and the glass slippers are beginning to pinch." She straightened. She knew what he wanted of her. "I guess we had better go back to playing at who we are."

He opened the door and held it for her. "Yes, we'd better."

It wasn't until later that he realized that he had agreed to her words, that he had admitted that he was pretending to be something he was not.

But which was the real Bryan Marlowe now? Bryan didn't have a clue.

Chapter Ten

The sound of the truck in the driveway piqued
Mike's interest enough to tear him away from the
video game he was playing in the family room. He
ran to the living-room window, which looked out onto
the driveway, passing his father on the sofa.

"Hey, Dad!" Mike tugged on the bottom of the
newspaper his father was reading. He pointed to the
window. "Look!"

Bryan did as he was told, although he knew what
to expect. It was a flatbed tow truck, its load a well-
polished automobile. Bryan and his son watched as
the driver of the truck unlatched the blue car and
backed it off the truck.

"Boy, what a neat car." Mike threw open the door
and ran out. In the driveway sat a gleaming metallic-
blue 1968 Mustang. "Is it ours?"

Bryan came up behind him. He took the clipboard
the driver motioned toward him and signed the necessary papers. "No, it's Kate's."

"Well, enjoy," the driver muttered as he got back into the cab of his truck. Slowly the tow truck pulled away.

Mike only had eyes for the car. "Katie's? I didn't know she had such a great car." He clambered into the driver's seat, then took hold of the steering wheel. He pretended to drive it, making a multitude of racing sounds to accompany himself.

"Wow."

Bryan peered into the car. "Careful, Ace, we don't want you running the car into the garage before Kate has a chance to see it."

Mike reluctantly let go of the steering wheel. "Does she know?"

"Know what?"

Mike climbed out of the car. "That her car's here," he said impatiently.

"It's a surprise, so I don't—" Bryan didn't get a chance to finish his sentence.

Mike dashed into the house, yelling, *"Katie, come quick!"* at the top of his lungs.

"And if that doesn't get the neighbors to complain, nothing will," Bryan murmured to himself as he leaned against the car, waiting.

Though he tried to rationalize that it was just a harmless whim on his part, Bryan could feel his anticipation rising as he waited to see Kate's reaction on being reunited with her beloved, though frequently disabled, car. He had found out from Molly that the car had been through three different owners, all family, and had been twice around the odometer. It was currently working on its third try at a hundred thousand miles. Now that he had had it outfitted with a new engine and a new transmission, Bryan thought, its chances of reaching that goal were a lot better.

Kate emerged from the house with Mike pulling impatiently on her arm. "What's all this about you having my car delivered?" she asked Bryan, confused.

And then she saw what he was leaning against. She stopped dead. Kate stared at the car in disbelief, then back at Bryan.

Bryan merely nodded, savoring the look on her face and his sense of satisfaction for having put it there. It had been a long time since giving a gift had given him this much pleasure.

Wordlessly Kate opened the glove compartment and saw her registration sitting on top of the map of L.A., just where she had left it. She closed the door and turned to look at Bryan.

"It *is* mine. How did it get here?"

"A big truck brought it, Katie," Mike told her, hopping around with excitement.

She gave him a small smile, but her eyes were on Bryan. "Why?"

Bryan shrugged, still leaning against the car, his arms crossed before him. "I thought you might like having your own car back. I had the transmission replaced, as well as the engine." He tried to gloss over the deed lightly now that it was out in the open. He had wanted to give her something, but everything he had thought of was much too personal, much too revealing. By doing this, he could hide behind some sort of practical explanation.

"Flowers would have been cheaper," she said softly.

"You can't drive flowers."

"No, you can't."

She was doing it again, seeing through him. Or at least, he thought so. Maybe he was giving her too much credit.

Lovingly she ran her hand along the hood. He had had the car polished as well, she noted. She looked at him. "I'm speechless."

"I doubt it."

"How did you know where to find it?"

"Speechless doesn't last long with you, does it?" He laughed. "Your aunt talks a lot, too. She told me all about your car. I thought since you've set my sons on the path of law and order, I might do something nice for you."

"You already have. You gave me a job and a place to stay."

Her wants certainly were simple. "Let's call it a bonus, then."

Kate whirled away from the car and threw her arms around his neck. "Oh, you are human, Bryan Marlowe, even though you don't want to admit it."

Almost without thinking, Bryan found himself holding her by the waist. It was as if he were programmed to respond to her and had no say in the matter, he thought.

Mike ran back to the entrance of the house. "Hey, guys, come quick, Kate and Dad are hugging!"

"That's bound to flush the neighbors out," Kate laughed, as unembarrassed as Bryan was flustered. Reluctantly she withdrew her arms. "How much did Bobby charge you?"

He almost drew her back against him, but stopped himself in time. It wasn't easy. "I said it was a gift."

"I can't accept something like this."

He had thought she'd love nothing better than having her car back in running order. "Why not?"

"Because it costs too much."

"Is that the only reason?"

She looked up at him innocently. "What other reason would there be?" She saw the turmoil and confusion in his eyes and wondered if she had blundered somehow. Maybe a gift of this magnitude didn't quite mean to him what it did to her. After all, he was very well-off.

"You are a dear, sweet man," she added quickly so that he wouldn't misunderstand, "but I'm used to paying my own way. Just your being thoughtful enough to ransom my car for me is gift enough. I'll pay you back."

"As you wish." He was disappointed, and yet, in a way, he wasn't. She *was* acting true to character. This would be, now that he thought about it, the way he would have expected her to react. She was, in all cases, her own woman. Maybe she was exactly what she seemed to be after all.

The triplets came running out into the driveway. They were far more taken with the car than with the vision of their father and Kate in an embrace.

"Hey!" cried Travis.

Trent circled it from the other side. "Wow!"

"Can we keep it?" They both asked at the same time.

"It's not ours, it's Katie's," Mike informed them importantly. "Dad gave it to her as a present."

"Does that mean you're going steady?" Trevor asked his father.

Kate came to Bryan's rescue. "No, that means I've got my car back from the shop, and your father's a very thoughtful man."

Kate sat down behind the steering wheel. It felt like a homecoming. And it was all because of him. He *did* care.

The boys tumbled into the car behind her.

"Can we go for a ride?" Travis urged.

"Please, Kate?" Trevor asked.

There were her studies to see to, but oh, the urge was great. Kate gave in. "Sure we can, after your father's gone through so much trouble for me." She looked up at him, her eyes shining.

"It wasn't—" he began.

"Oh yes it was," Kate laughed. "C'mon, get in if you're game."

"I," he protested teasingly for the benefit of his sons, "am always game."

"Nice to know, Mr. Marlowe, nice to know."

The smile she gave him made Bryan feel warm and alive.

They drove through the development and took a tour of Beverly Hills before Kate reluctantly called a halt to the excursion. They returned to the house just in time to hear the phone ring.

"I'll get it," Kate called out. She flashed Bryan a warm smile as he walked past her to settle back on the sofa with his newspaper. "Marlowe residence. Oh, hello." She was about to call Bryan to the telephone when the person on the other end of the line stopped her. "What? Yes, fine, of course, I'll tell him.

Eight sharp.'' She hung up and turned to find Bryan studying her.

"Friend of yours?" he asked.

"No, friend of yours. That was Mrs. Howell. She apologizes for such short notice, but she's throwing a party tomorrow night for a Judge Neighbors who's dropped into town unexpectedly. She requests your presence."

"You said no." But he knew she hadn't.

"I know for a fact that you're free tomorrow. I said yes."

"Why didn't you give me the telephone?"

"Because she asked that the request be relayed to you. I guess she thinks that if you don't talk to her in person, you can't turn her down."

"Then she has another think coming." Bryan rose and crossed to Kate. He picked up the phone and began to dial.

"You're canceling?"

"I'm canceling."

Kate put her hand over his. The contact was intimate. It always seemed to be. That was her gift and his curse, that she could draw a person out with a touch, a word. "Bryan," she lowered her voice, allowing herself the luxury of calling him by his first name when no one else was listening, "you don't get out enough. Enough? You don't get out at all."

"Kate," he began patiently, "I'd like to remind you that my social situation is none of your concern."

She took no offense. He was just stubborn. She understood stubborn. She had been raised with it. Her mother had accused her of being that way on occasion, although Kate never noticed it. "Oh, but it is. I need to generate a healthy atmosphere for the boys if I'm to promote their well-being.''

"More child psych?"

"Child experience is more like it." She thought of her own family.

"And you think that if I went to Alexis's party with some voluptuous woman on my arm, my sons will grow up well adjusted?"

She discovered that she didn't particularly like that image. She had thought of him going by himself and spending the evening with friends. "That's not quite what I meant. I'm just trying to fill your life out a little."

You've already done that. More than you'll ever know, Kate, more than you'll ever know. He made a quick decision before he had time to think it through. "All right, I'll go."

"Good." But then she couldn't help adding, "With a voluptuous woman on your arm?"

His eyes slid over her body, and Kate felt familiar stirrings.

"That depends."

"On what?"

"On whether you consider yourself in that category."

"Me?" There was no keeping the surprised pleasure from her eyes or her voice.

Bryan turned and walked back to the sofa. "You got me into this, it's only fitting that you suffer along with me."

"I'll try to bear up to it." She began to head toward the stairs and her textbooks, then hesitated at the first step. "As long as you're sure."

Bryan looked at her over the top of the newspaper. "I'm sure."

What he was sure of, actually, was that he was plotting his own downfall. He knew that disaster and disappointment lay at the end of the trail he was treading, and yet, he couldn't stop it from happening. His best efforts to save himself kept evaporating whenever he thought of Kate. She brought sunshine into his life, laughter, not to mention what a whiz she was with his sons. He *wanted* to take her out, *wanted* to be with her as much as possible.

He was a man, Bryan told himself as he watched her walk up the stairs, appreciating the gentle sway of her hips, who didn't seem to learn from his mistakes. He was setting himself up for a fall.

He was already falling, he realized the next night. He was falling in love with this Irish tornado named Kate who had blown into his life.

He was ready early and was waiting for her in the family room, playing a game of dominoes with his sons to keep his mind off the eventual consequences of his actions.

He looked at her as she came down the stairs. The dress she wore, a shade of gray-blue, was simple, yet beautiful. Everything that came in contact with her was somehow made beautiful. He knew she brought out the best in him. Away from her, his dark thoughts crowded his mind. But when he was near her, they dissipated.

Kate crossed into the room. The boys were all hunched over the coffee table, each with his own set of pieces. Kate took in the scene, and it made her feel warm. A man who loved his sons this much could definitely be reached, she told herself. It was only a matter of time. And, she reminded herself, thinking of the car, she was already making great strides toward that end.

She placed a hand on Trent's shoulder, but addressed Bryan. "I take it by your expression that I look all right."

He laughed. "Nothing backward and shy about you, is there?"

"Not to my knowledge. Would you rather I were?"

"No." It was the truth. He didn't want her any other way than what she was. But would she remain that way? Or was it all just an illusion, born of his rebelling desire? Old fears died hard.

"Then isn't it lucky I'm not?"

No, not for me. For me, Bryan thought, it's going to be my downfall.

It was clear that the game was over. Mike and Trent let their pieces fall, face down.

Trevor rose to his feet. "Where are you and Dad going?"

She looked down at the serious face. He always seemed so worried that he was going to be left behind. She wondered what it would take to make him more secure. She cupped his small chin in her hand, her fingers gentle. "To a party, honey."

Bryan held up his hands. "Don't blame me, guys, it's Kate's fault. She's the one who said yes to the invitation. I'd much rather stay here."

"Can we come?" Travis wanted to know.

Bryan shook his head. "Not this time." He and

Kate crossed to the front door with their animated escort. "This is for grown-ups."

"But we'll all go out next weekend," Kate promised as they slipped out the door.

"We will?" Bryan took her arm. Funny how natural all this was becoming. He had to steel himself against it from becoming too natural, too easy. It would be so much harder to backtrack then.

Maybe it was already too late.

He led her over to the Mercedes. "This way they have something to look forward to," she told him.

Bryan held the door open for her. "And what do I have to look forward to?"

She sat down, then swung her legs in. She was aware of the fact that he was looking at them. It made her tingle. "A nice evening."

"For that, I'd have to stay home." He came around the other side and got in.

She waited until he started up the car. "Don't you like going out and mingling?"

"I used to."

"But?"

He kept his face forward, not trusting himself to look at her. "Let's drop it."

She held her hands up. "Dropped."

But as they drove, she couldn't help wondering about the subject. Why wouldn't he open up and tell her? It would do him good. It would do her good, as well, she mused. She wanted to glimpse a bigger slice of his past than he was allowing her to see. It wasn't right to shut people out this way. Had he been totally destroyed by his wife's death? Would she never be able to reach him for more than a few short moments at a time?

Outwardly he seemed to have gone on with his life, but if he had, why weren't there any women in it? He was more than just a mildly attractive man. He was ruggedly handsome. And there was a magnetism about him, a subtle sensuality that wove its way deeper and deeper into her senses every time she was around him.

She was oddly quiet tonight, Bryan thought as he spared her a glance while waiting for the light to change at the intersection. He liked the way the moonlight shone on her hair, making it appear to be spun silver.

Was he crazy? Here was a beautiful woman who was warm and witty and fun, and he was putting up barricades between them. Barricades, he reminded himself, that she kept breaking through. Was that just because she was persistent, or because he wanted her to break through any obstacles. Or both?

"We're here," he said needlessly as they came to a stop at the curb.

She barely glanced at the huge house. "I recognize it," Kate said quietly.

"That's right, you were here before. This is where we met. I forgot."

She knew he hadn't. Why did he feel the need to back away from even the slightest intimacy with her?

"I thought lawyers never forgot anything."

"If that were true, I would have remembered to stick to my principles," he muttered.

She knew he hadn't meant for her to hear, but she

wanted him to clarify what he was thinking. "Which are?"

He held open the door for her and she got out. "Never mind." Placing his hand on the small of her back, he escorted Kate to the Howells' front door.

Alexis opened the door and gave Bryan a cheery smile and then looked Kate over with mild curiosity. Kate could tell she was trying to place her. She hadn't looked nearly this sophisticated the last time she was here.

"Bryan, you really did come." Alexis put her arm through Bryan's and led him inside. "Jeremy and I have a bet going. He said that you'd never show. I said you would. I like winning." She peered around him to look at Kate. "And who's this?"

"My governess." Bryan realized how inane that sounded as soon as he said it.

"Really, Bryan," Alexis purred, "I scarcely thought you needed one, but, whatever it takes to get you out of your shell." She waved her hand airily. "Come, you know everyone here."

Still holding his arm solicitously, the woman led him into the living room. Bryan made a grab for Kate's hand and pulled her along in his wake. Kate suppressed a smile. She took his action as an indication that he needed her.

If he had harbored any apprehensions about Kate not fitting in with his friends, he should have known better. She didn't just fit in, she held court. As he watched her mingle with the other people at the party that evening, Bryan saw that she charmed not only the men but the women, as well. And he grew conscious of something else. He was proud of the way people responded to her. He was proud of her. It was the kind of pride that spelled danger.

"The worst thing a man can do is give up drinking."

Bryan turned to see Angus Hitchcock behind him, nursing a tall glass of mineral water. The senior partner of the prestigious law firm held his glass aloft. "My doctor's idea. He said I'd live longer." Angus made a dour face. "I won't live longer. It'll only *feel* longer." The old man looked off at a small circle of people over in the corner. Kate was at its center. "I see the new woman is really working out."

"Yes, she is."

Angus looked knowingly at Bryan. With a gnarled hand, he patted Bryan's shoulder. "Glad to hear that, Bryan. Charmed the pants off me. If I were twenty years younger, hell, maybe thirty, I'd give you a run for your money."

"I was referring to her working out as the boys' governess."

There was an amused glint in the old man's eye. "I wasn't." He wove his way through the crowd, chuckling.

"Now aren't you glad I accepted the invitation for you?" Kate asked as they drove home in his car. "Admit it, you had a good time."

"Guilty. But only because—"

Kate turned around in her seat to see him more clearly. "Because?" she encouraged.

He didn't feel like lying. "Because you were there.

You have a way of lighting things up, Kate.'' My life, for instance, he added silently.

"Like a lightning rod," she laughed softly, refusing to let the conversation become too serious. She knew that whenever it did, she lost him. He got that faraway look in his eyes, and then there was distance between them again. She didn't want distance, especially not now. She wanted warmth and laughter. Most of all, she realized, she wanted him to kiss her, here and now, to make her feel that way she yearned to feel with a man, with him. "Bryan?"

"Yes?"

"Could you stop the car and pull over?"

They were almost home. "Why?" Was she ill?

"Because if I kiss you while you're driving, you might crash this nice car of yours."

He pulled over to the side. A warm sensuality pulsated through him, and he wanted nothing more than to hold her in his arms. "You are a thoughtful creature, Kate."

"So I've been told." She paused. "You know, Bryan, I've never been accused of being a shy, retiring sort."

"Not in this lifetime."

She smiled softly. "But it really would be nice if you made a few moves of your own."

Gently he touched first her forehead, then her temples, with his lips. Kate felt herself melting inside. "This to your liking?"

"Very much so." She opened her eyes and searched his face, looking for something she wasn't quite sure of yet, a sign perhaps. She smiled at him, her eyes smoky with desire. "I knew all you needed was a bit of coaxing."

Bryan caressed her cheek gently with the edge of his knuckle. "And you can do that."

"With the best of them. But that's not all I'm good at."

"Not," he drew her near again, "by a long shot."

As he pulled her close, the stick shift got in the way. She looked at it accusingly. "You'd think that a car made in Europe would be more conducive to romance, wouldn't you?"

He wanted to make love to her more than he wanted anything else at that moment, perhaps at any single moment of his life. But it was wrong, wrong for him. Getting involved led to a myriad of things that he didn't want. It led to disappointments and heartache. He had had more than his share.

He leaned his forehead against hers. "Yes, you'd think that. I suppose that's why they make back-seats."

But she knew from his tone that he wasn't suggesting anything so impulsive. His tone told her that the heat of the moment had passed. Control was back. That damnable control of his that held her at arm's length and caused him to retreat into a land where she couldn't follow.

What makes you tick, Bryan Marlowe? Where did all this hurt come from and why won't you open up to me?

Aloud, she said, "It's getting late and you've a day in court tomorrow."

He started up the car again. "Um, yes. And you have classes." The words were agonizingly formal, a complete contrast to what had transpired between them only a moment ago.

A shaft of pain went through her. Was she just imagining that he wanted her? Was she blinded by her own reaction to him? "Yes, I have classes," she echoed.

They drove the rest of the way in silence.

When they arrived home, she opened the door on her side, not wanting anything from him, not even the slightest gesture of gallantry. It was small and petty, she thought, but she couldn't help herself. The man had hurt her even if he hadn't meant to.

Bryan came to then. He got out, coming around to her side in time to hold the door as she got out. She rose, her body held in check so not to touch his. He recognized the effort on her part, saw the fleeting glimpse of hurt in her eyes. He reached out and touched her face.

"Kate."

A tiny flare of hope rose. God, would she never give up? "Yes?"

He dropped his hand to his side. Don't start, don't start, he warned himself. You'll both only regret it in the end. "Nothing."

She wanted to shake him, to make him talk to her, to make the words that he was withholding pour out. Instead, she nodded and turned toward the door. Maybe she should have taken adult psychology instead.

Chapter Eleven

How come you're making dinner, Katie?" Trevor asked as he balanced himself on a stool adjacent to the work counter in the kitchen. He was intently watching Kate's every move.

Kate paused, pushed her bangs out of her eyes, then continued mashing potatoes in a large metal pot. "Because Molly isn't feeling well today."

Trevor peered into the rectangular dish on the counter, which contained sautéed beef covered with peas and strips of mozzarella cheese. "What's that?" he asked.

"Shepherd's pie." She liberally spread the mashed potatoes over the combination.

"Why's it called shepherd's pie? Do you have to be a shepherd to eat it?" Trevor propped his elbows up on the counter and rested his chin between his hands. Behind him, Travis marched in.

"No, dummy. Stop asking so many questions,"

Travis taunted his brother. He took a can of soda out of the refrigerator.

"Well now, there's nothing wrong with questions, Travis. That's how you learn." Kate wiped her hands on her apron. "Right, Trevor?"

"Right." He nodded his head with satisfaction at his sibling.

Travis shrugged and went off to play in the next room. But Trevor chose to remain with Kate.

Nothing pleased her more than the way the boy had blossomed since she had come to stay at the house. His reticent behavior was nearly gone. He now held his own with his brothers. If nothing else, she could be proud of that, she told herself. Now, if only she could find a way to help his father.

Mentally she shrugged in frustration. But not in surrender.

"Trevor, I need some aluminum foil, please."

He made a beeline for the pantry, happy to be of service. He laid the long box on the counter. "You know what, Katie?"

"What, Trevor?" She pulled out a long piece of foil, cut it and covered the baking dish.

"I wish my Mama could have met you." He climbed back on the stool that stood at the cooking island opposite Kate. Somewhat precariously he perched forward on his knees. "I know she would have liked you."

"Why, thank you." Kate placed the pan into the oven and set the timer. She turned back to face Trevor. "Do you remember much about your mother?" She maintained a casual tone. She felt that he needed to face his mother's death at his own speed. He needed to unleash the pain that resided within him.

Trevor thought for a moment. "A little. She was pretty and smelled good, like you do. 'Cept I don't think she laughed much."

"Well, taking care of four boys is a big responsibility. Maybe she didn't have much time to laugh." Kate hung the apron on a hook inside the pantry door.

"You do."

She settled down on the stool next to him. "I'm different. I need to laugh. Laughter's like sunshine for me. I need a little every day. You can put the aluminum foil away now."

He did as he was told. She watched as he solemnly carried out the task. "You know, you're a lot more helpful than my brothers were. I had a lot of trouble getting them to mind me."

The pantry door closed with a loud bang as he released it. "I like listening to you." And then his sunny expression clouded over. "Katie?"

She had gotten her sweatshirt dirty despite the apron. Kate rose to go and change. "What, honey?"

"You're never gonna go on a plane, are you?"

His question made her stop and turn around. "Well, I wasn't planning on it. Why?"

"'Cause my Mama did, with my Daddy, and then she never came back."

She could see his eyes suddenly shine with unshed tears. She walked around the counter, knelt down and took him into her arms. "No plane rides, Trevor, I promise."

He buried his face in her neck and sighed.

* * *

"Why Kate, how lovely to see you. Won't you come in?" Bryan's mother stepped back and gestured her unexpected visitor into the small, tidy living room.

Kate walked in. She had just dropped off the boys at school, and today her first class was at ten. Yesterday's conversation with Trevor had left her unsettled. And this morning, rather than head straight for the campus, she stopped at Mrs. Marlowe's house. There were answers she had to have.

She looked at the gray-haired woman. "I hope you don't mind me dropping by."

"Why no, I've been meaning to stop by and see you myself." Mrs. Marlowe led Kate into the kitchen.

She reminded Kate a little of her own mother, except perhaps, that she was a bit softer-looking. Moira Llewellyn had had to be tougher. There was so much that could have broken both her spirit and her will if she hadn't been. Alicia Marlowe was a product of genteel upbringing.

"Oh?" Kate asked. "What about?"

They entered the cheery yellow-wallpapered kitchen. Mrs. Marlowe gestured toward a chair at the small table. "I wanted to thank you, dear."

Kate sat down, tucking her legs to the side. She watched her hostess with a growing curiosity. "Thank me? For what?"

"For being Kate, I suppose. Goodness," she waved her hand, flustered, "I do express myself badly. Bryan has the golden tongue in our family, I'm afraid. How does tea sound?"

Though Kate's Irish family had remained devoted tea-drinkers, Kate had always hated the stuff. Still,

she wanted badly to be polite. She made sure to keep
the grimace she made inwardly from reaching her
face. "Sounds wonderful."

Mrs. Marlowe flitted about the kitchen while Kate
waited patiently for a further explanation.

"There." Mrs. Marlowe set down a silver tray with
a teapot, then sat down herself. "Need cream?
Sugar?"

Nothing could help tea taste better as far as she
was concerned. "This is fine," Kate assured her.

Mrs. Marlowe poured, then leaned forward in her
chair. The fine porcelain cup rattled a little against the
saucer as she lifted it up in both hands. She took a
sip, then set it down again. For a moment, Mrs. Marlowe toyed with the rim. "He's happier, you know.
Bryan, I mean. And the boys, too. You've been wonderful for them all, Kate."

"Well, the boys have settled down a bit, and we
do get on very well. But as for himself—" Kate
stopped as she heard herself use the old-world reference to the head of the household. "As for your
son—"

Mrs. Marlowe anticipated Kate's next statement.
She waved her hand at the words. "You've done him
a world of good, too. He's happier than I've seen him
in a long, long time."

"Happier?" Kate cried incredulously. Not in her
book. That was just the problem. "Mrs. Marlowe, that
man is remote, standoffish—just when I think I can
get him to open up, snap—" she clapped her hands
together "—the gate comes down, and he's away
again."

Mrs. Marlowe nodded philosophically. Kate could

see that her words had no effect on the conclusion the woman had drawn about her influence on Bryan. "The plane crash is something that's hard for him to talk about or even deal with."

Now they were coming to the heart of the matter. She was relieved that Mrs. Marlowe had brought it up first. Kate became more animated. "Then she did die in a plane crash. Trevor said something about his mother going off with Mr. Marlowe and not coming back. Was he hurt in the crash, too?"

Mrs. Marlowe shook her head. "He wasn't on that flight, thank heavens. I don't know why, but Jill took an earlier flight back—"

"To come home to the boys?" Kate guessed. She took a sip of tea, not wanting to insult Mrs. Marlowe.

"Oh, I doubt that." The older woman clucked, dismissing the suggestion. "Don't misunderstand," she continued hastily, "my late daughter-in-law wasn't a bad mother. At least, not by conscious choice. Before the children came along, Jill used to coo at all the babies she saw. But I think her own made her rather...nervous, uncomfortable, so to speak. No, that last trip he and Jill took was Bryan's idea. He thought Jill needed to get away for a little while."

Then the rest of it didn't make any sense. "Then why was she returning home without him? If she was as 'uncomfortable' as you say, I would've thought that she would have wanted to stay away as long as possible."

The older woman shook her head. "I don't know. I could never get myself to ask Bryan. It upset him so. But I do know that he blamed himself for her death. He let it eat at him. For the first two weeks after the crash, I was afraid that he wouldn't come around.'' She folded her hands before her and looked down at them contemplatively, remembering what it had been like.

Then her expression grew lighter as she smiled. ''But then, of course, there were the boys. They needed him, and he knew he wasn't alone in his grief.'' She sighed. ''But he changed after that. He wasn't my lighthearted Bryan any more. He stopped laughing, stopped seeing people socially. He was always a great socializer,'' she confided. ''So was Jill. Perhaps that's why he stopped. Maybe the memory was too painful for him.''

''And he doesn't go out?'' Her assumption had been correct.

''Not at all. Oh, to functions he can't get out of, because of his firm, or important clients. But other than that, no. And he hasn't seen any woman other than on a business basis. But he does smile when he speaks of you, Kate.'' She leaned forward, and with two frail hands she clasped Kate's. ''I had a feeling you'd be good for him the first time I saw you, Kate. I'm rarely wrong in my intuitions.''

Kate smiled gently at Mrs. Marlowe's seriousness.

''Bear with him a little longer, dear.''

She was asking her to stay just as Trevor had. It certainly did make a person feel wanted, Kate thought.

''I've no plans to go anywhere, Mrs. Marlowe. The boys are dear to me and I love being with them.''

''And Bryan?''

''He's my employer.''

But Mrs. Marlowe wouldn't let it rest. "And nothing more?"

Kate pushed aside the half-empty cup. "He won't let it be anything more, Mrs. Marlowe."

Mrs. Marlowe pressed her lips together, disappointed but not put off. "I never knew my son to be a fool, Kate. He'll come around. Now then, what did you want to see me about?"

"Just a little friendly conversation," Kate lied, surprised with herself. She had never felt the need to lie about things before. What was it about Bryan that turned everything so topsy-turvy for her?

"More tea?" Mrs. Marlowe offered.

Kate smiled and pushed her cup forward. She had lied, she thought philosophically, and now this was penance. She took it stoically.

"I spoke to my mother today," Bryan said as soon as Kate walked into his den that evening. He had worked hard to curb his annoyance all through dinner. He wanted her alone when he brought up the matter, not with a support team surrounding her. "And she mentioned that you had dropped by. Why?"

Kate didn't like the quiet tone in his voice. He sounded like a warrior preparing to go into battle. She knew what was coming. He didn't want her probing into his life. But she couldn't help if she couldn't probe. And she wanted to help, wanted it very, very much.

Kate didn't take her customary seat. Instead, she stood next to it, her gaze wary. "I had some questions to ask her."

"Why didn't you come to me with them?" It was a rhetorical question. He already knew why.

She refused to look away, even though she didn't like the anger in his eyes. "Because you wouldn't have answered them."

"Then perhaps," he said heatedly, "they shouldn't have been asked."

His waking vulnerability around Kate had been tormenting him for some time now, and it came to a head this afternoon when he had discovered, quite by chance, that Kate had come to his mother and asked about him. About the past. He didn't want her knowing, didn't want her any closer than she was already. Closeness bred pain, and he didn't want that, didn't want the penalties that it exacted. He'd built a wall around himself, had structured his life to the point that he could now cope with life. But it was a delicate structure, and Kate threatened to bring it tumbling down around him.

Kate put her hands on the back of the chair and leaned slightly forward. "They had to be asked if I was going to help you."

"Help me?" He raised his voice. "Lady, you haven't got your degree yet, and if you did, it would only qualify you to work with children."

"Children aren't the only ones who hurt," she pointed out, raising her voice.

Bryan slammed shut the book he was paging through. "Ms. Llewellyn, I think that's quite enough."

Kate raised herself up on her toes. "Oh, it's Ms. Llewellyn now, is it? Well, it wasn't Ms. Llewellyn when you kissed me."

"You kissed me," he reminded her. There was a wall of anger rising within him, making him say things he knew hurt her. He hated himself for it, but couldn't stop.

The reminder that she had had to initiate the action stung, as did his flinging it back at her. "You kissed back! And you told me things with that kiss that you wouldn't say with words."

She was shouting at him. Bryan rose to regain leverage. "So now you analyze kisses. You might open up a whole new world of psychiatry. Kiss interpretations. Anything like dream analysis?"

That did it. The temper she had worked so hard to keep sheathed erupted, bringing with it the Irish brogue that always surfaced when she was agitated. "You are the world's most pig-headed man! Are you some kind of deity that you can't be admittin' that you're human, that you can't be askin' for help from another human being?"

"When and if I need help, I'll ask for it."

"You *are* askin' for it," she insisted. "But you're just too stubborn to say it aloud. It's in your eyes."

"Ah, my eyes and my lips." His voice was cold, sarcastic. "Anywhere else? My hair for instance?"

"I've never told an employer what an idiot he was before, but Mr. Bryan Marlowe, I'm comin' very, very close to startin' a precedent." She clenched her fists at her sides. She knew if she stayed, it would be disastrous for them both. "If you'll excuse me, I have to be attendin' to my studies now."

With that, she went out and slammed the door in her wake.

The paperweight on Bryan's desk shook and nearly

fell off. He muttered an oath as he made a grab for it. He had an urge to throw it, but he didn't. Instead, he replaced it on his desk.

Damn.

She had no business meddling in his affairs, in his past. It was his burden to keep, his to learn from.

And what have you learned? he mocked himself. You're still dreaming dreams.

He looked at the closed door. Not anymore.

Breakfast the next morning was tense and silent, despite Kate's best efforts. She heaped a sum of silent Irish curses on Bryan's head for having reduced her to this. Why, oh why couldn't he come to his senses? Why wouldn't he let her help?

Why wouldn't he let her in?

The boys noticed the change immediately. Although she spoke to them the way she always did, she didn't address Bryan at all. Since Molly was still in bed, the last to be felled by the flu that had been ricocheting around the household, Kate was serving breakfast. The boys all got their favorite. Bryan got what, in her estimation, he deserved.

He poked at the lump on his plate with his fork. "The eggs are cold," he informed Kate sharply.

She made no move to remove them or get him another serving. "They're not the only thing," she answered, looking at him pointedly.

"Katie?" Trent tried to say her name with his mouth full of pancakes.

"Swallow first, Trent," Kate prompted. "I won't have you choking to death. It'll dampen the rest of my day. Now—'' she saw that he had swallowed ''—what is it?'' She took a sip of coffee.

''Did you and Dad get married last night?''

She almost spit out her coffee. ''What?'' Out of the corner of her eye, she saw that Bryan had much the same reaction to the innocent, out-of-left-field question.

''Did you and Dad get married last night?''

''What makes you think that?'' she cried.

''Well, you're not really talking to each other anymore, you're just kinda snapping,'' Mike explained his younger brother's words.

Kate exchanged glances with Bryan. So this is how his marriage had appeared to them, she thought. Very edifying. It hadn't been all happiness the way she had believed. Bryan's behavior was becoming more mysterious.

''No, we didn't get married last night,'' Bryan told his sons. He had been wrong to snap at her the way he had, and he knew it. He had been looking for a way out of the emotional whirlpool she had sucked him into. Driving her away seemed to be his only recourse. Except that he couldn't follow through. ''Your Dad just got up on the wrong side of the bed this morning.''

''What side was that, Dad?'' Travis asked.

''Was it on Kate's side?'' Trent wanted to know.

Kate shook her head and laughed. Bryan joined her. For the moment, peace was restored between them.

But she couldn't help wondering how soon and when it was going to disintegrate again. For she meant to dig deeper, whether or not he wanted her to. She was committed to it, not just because she felt he was suffering, but because she knew that there could be nothing between them, ever, unless the past was cleared away and put in its proper place.

That there was going to be a future for them she never doubted. Some things she just knew.

Chapter Twelve

Bryan wearily opened the front door and promptly stumbled over a rolled-up tent that was inadvertently blocking the doorway. He grabbed the doorjamb in order to keep from pitching forward into the foyer. Startled, he looked around. The entire foyer and living room looked like the outdoor-living department of a sporting-goods store.

"What's all this?" He dropped his attaché case next to a stack of cooking utensils.

Kate was winding up her inventory, checking that nothing had been overlooked. She glanced in Bryan's direction. "It's Friday."

Another circular route to the final answer. Bryan sighed, searching for patience. It had been an unusually trying week at work for him. "Yes, I know it's Friday. But that doesn't explain the camping gear."

"Isn't this neat, Dad?" Mike shouted from a corner of the living room as he rolled up his sleeping bag. The triplets were struggling with theirs.

Kate made her way over to the boys. "Your mother told me that you used to like to go camping to unwind."

"Yes, but—" With a look of defeat, Bryan surrendered, leaned against the wall and waited for the scenario to unfold.

Kate finished rolling Trevor's sleeping bag and went on to Trent's. "And I thought you might like to unwind after your hectic week."

Bryan only half listened as she animatedly proceeded to defend her position. His mind kept drifting, inspired by the gentle sway of her hips as she moved about. He could think of better ways than camping to ease the tension he felt. He caught himself mentally undressing her. Yes, there were definitely better ways than camping.

Kate turned to see Bryan watching her. The look in his eyes startled her. His mind wasn't on the subject. He probably wasn't listening to a word she was saying. "Mr. Marlowe, you're not paying attention to me."

"More than you'll ever know, Kate," he murmured. He cut his mental wanderings short. "Who told you I had a hectic week?"

"Sylvia," she said simply, naming his secretary as an accomplice.

Bryan saw Travis struggling and moved over to the boy to help him with his sleeping bag. "You called." It wasn't a question. By now, it was an assumption.

"I called."

Might as well go with it. His weariness was beginning to fade at that. Maybe a camping trip wouldn't be so bad after all. "Were there any hurricanes named Kate the night you were born?"

Kate smiled, satisfied with herself. The tone of his voice told her he was receptive to her plan. Convincing him had been easier than she had thought. "My mother told me it was a calm night. Why?"

"I thought perhaps you might be a changeling."

She paused. Had she made a mistake after all? "You don't want to go camping?"

"Why, Dad, why?" The triplets crowded around him.

"You're going so fast," Bryan told Kate. "I'm not sure what I want." Yes I do, he thought. You. He knew she could read the desire in his eyes. And he didn't look away.

The children, oblivious to what was going on, surrounded their father. "Please, Dad. Can we go?"

"Can we?"

"We haven't been camping for soooo long."

He tousled Trent's head. "Sure, we can go."

Kate let out a sigh. She'd been right after all. "Fine. I've got all the cooking paraphernalia I need, so I'd better start packing it all up."

Bryan disengaged himself from his sons, each of whom was intent on hugging him the hardest. "You're coming along?" He looked at Kate in mild surprise.

She didn't understand his reaction. Was he trying to exclude her? She felt a momentary pang at the rejection. "Of course I'm coming along. It was my idea."

"It's just that my wife never—" Jill hated camping. It was another thing he discovered that they differed on. He assumed that Kate was doing it out of a sense of obligation. "You don't have to, you know."

"I know." She put down the frying pan she was packing. "You don't seem to understand, Mr. Marlowe. I *want* to go camping."

"You've been before?" He grinned, intrigued.

She laughed, and a mischievous look entered her eyes. "Is there a pot of gold at the end of the rainbow?"

And with that enigmatic question, she left the room.

"If she weren't so tall, I'd swear she was a leprechaun," Bryan muttered under his breath, shaking his head.

The idea did sound good to him. Getting away from the pressures of the city, out in the open with his sons, would help him unwind. He looked over to the doorway where she had disappeared. She always seemed to be one step ahead of him. Funny thing, he was getting rather used to it. And liking it. He also like the idea of her coming along.

But he still had his doubts about her camping abilities when they set out the next morning. Her answer about the pot of gold led him to cynically believe that she had never gone camping. However, on reconsideration, he realized that to her way of thinking, she probably *believed* that there was a pot of gold at the end of the rainbow, which means she had gone camping.

All in all, she was an extraordinary woman.

And, if she had never been camping before, Bryan thought later that day, he would have never been able to guess it. She could backpack and tramp through the woods with the best of them.

Better than that, she could bait hooks.

When Trevor closed his eyes, unable to push a worm onto a hook, she did it for him, fabricating a story about an ancient spell that had been cast upon all worms, preserving them from feeling any sort of pain when they were used by fishermen. Trevor looked relieved and settled back to enjoy the fishing after that.

"Fish psychology now?" Bryan asked as she sat down next to him on the riverbank.

"I've found that a bit of blarney carefully placed can do a lot of good." She cast her own line into the still waters.

"What's blarney, Katie?" Travis asked, overhearing.

"The gift of words, son," Bryan said.

She leaned in toward him and whispered, "Thank you, Mr. Marlowe"

"You're welcome, Ms. Llewellyn." He grinned at her. He couldn't help himself. Bryan felt warmed by more than just the sunshine.

The afternoon slipped away pleasantly, with a little talking, a little fishing, and a general feeling of time-lessness and well-being. Bryan spent most of that time lying back on the grassy bank, his pole propped up, content just with being next to her, listening to her talk to the boys. She made him feel like a kid again. Well, not quite a kid, he reflected, but as carefree as he had been in his early twenties, when he had been in love, and the world—

Appalled, Bryan came to an abrupt mental halt.

When had love entered into it? It was the wrong word. It—

It was the right word and he knew it, no matter how much he fought it, God help him. Now that he had admitted it to himself, he had to do something about it. He couldn't let things slide any longer.

Kate could feel Bryan's mood shift, though not a word was spoken. "You're getting that strange look in your eye again," she observed aloud. It was the look that told her he was slipping away from her, back to whatever it was that held him in its grip.

He rose suddenly. "I think we've caught enough fish for today, boys. Time to clean them and have supper."

Kate got to her feet, as well, brushing off her jeans. He had changed the subject, and she knew there was no use pursuing the matter. "Division of labor," she announced to Bryan. "You clean, I cook."

"What'll we do, Katie?" Trevor asked.

It still amazed Bryan that the boys were so eager to help, but he saw that Kate took it in stride. She put her arm around Trevor. "You can rinse off the plates in the stream when we're done." They walked back to the campgrounds.

"Squeamish?" Bryan noticed that she averted her eyes as he gutted the trout.

She saw no reason to hide her aversion. "I barely passed high-school biology. I set the frog free."

Yes, he could see her doing that. With her bright outlook, she undoubtedly believed that everything had a right to live, to flourish. Was that what she was trying to do with him? Make him flourish? He didn't doubt it. At times, he felt as if she were succeeding. But those were times when reality and the past temporarily slipped his mind.

Temporarily, but not for long.

After dinner was done and the dishes all cleared away, Kate took out the guitar she had lugged all the way into the campgrounds. He had teased her about being a troubadour while they hiked, but now, as she played, he recalled how charmed he had been by her voice. She began to play a rousing tune and called for them to join her. The boys did so with no hesitation.

After a chorus had gone by, Kate looked in Bryan's direction. "I don't hear a baritone."

Bryan leaned back against a tree, his hands laced behind his head. "And you won't."

Kate strummed softly. "Don't tell me you don't sing."

"All right, I won't tell you."

She couldn't let it die there. "Everyone can sing."

"But not on key."

"That's all right—" she accepted his explanation, but didn't excuse him "—just make it loud. C'mon," she urged, "it's fun."

There was no arguing with her. There never seemed to be. He gave up. "You asked for it." Bryan sang, as promised, off-key. Kate's voice blended with his, and she carried him, carried them all. As he took note of that, he realized that was the pattern things had settled into.

They sang song after song. Each time she stopped, the boys begged her for just one more.

"All right, but this is the last 'just one more.'

When it's finished, it's off to bed with you." She looked at the semicircle of small faces.

"Promise."

"Sure, Katie."

"Just one more."

With a knowing gleam in her eye, Kate strummed softly. She sang "An Irish Lullaby", and Bryan felt a mellowness come over him, enveloping him. Content just to sit and listen to her, he didn't realize until she was through that the boys had drifted off to sleep.

"Very clever," he told her in a whisper.

"I thought so." She raised the guitar strap from her shoulder and laid the instrument aside. "Now, if you'll be so kind as to carry your sons into the tent one by one, I'll tuck them into the sleeping bags. Wake them and *you* get to sing them to sleep."

"No thanks."

Only Mike offered any protest, and that was half-hearted as his lids fell down heavily again over his eyes.

Kate tucked his arms into the sleeping bag. "Hush now, Mike. You need your rest." She sank back on her heels. The boy was asleep. "And so do we," she added in a whisper.

She came out of the tent. "Well, that's all of them." She joined Bryan at the camp fire. It blazed brightly, casting a warm glow around them. She ran her hands up and down her arms. The night air had turned brisk. "It's a fine lot of sons you have, Bryan Marlowe."

"I know it. Cold?"

"Just a little."

Without thinking, he slipped his arm around her.

She laid her head on his shoulder, not saying anything, content in enjoying the preciousness of the moment.

"I'm sorry I snapped at you the other night."

She raised her head, amusement shining in her eyes. "Which snap was that?"

He wound a lock of her hair around his finger. It felt so soft, so silky, just as she did, he thought. "The one that made you yell at me."

Kate moved nearer still, enjoying the intimacy of their closeness. "Oh, that time. I've a temper, I'm afraid."

"I hadn't noticed until then."

"I've been trying extra hard."

"And I haven't." He wasn't baiting her. It was a fact and they both knew it.

"Oh, I don't know about that. You're coming along. You smile more now than you did when I first came. It becomes you, you know. Makes you look like your sons. Innocent." She regarded his face, and need rose to the fore. Her eyes touched his mouth. "Well, maybe not too innocent," she whispered.

The light of the camp fire added a glow to her face and kissed her lips. And so did he.

This time, the passion was there immediately, only waiting for a chance to ignite. He hungered for her, hungered for the life-giving sweetness that only she seemed to possess. His body heated just at the mere touch of her mouth.

He slid his hands beneath her sweater. Again she shivered, but this time he knew it wasn't from the cold. It matched a kindred reaction within him. Desire. Anticipation. His fingers gently spanned the small circumference of her waist and moved upward. He felt her twist against him, felt her mouth grow more insistent. Could her impish way also harbor something so very raw, so very basic?

Could she want him as much as he did her? He didn't think it was possible.

Kate felt her pulse race until it become a hammering rhythm that echoed in her body. It matched the throbbing impatience she felt within her loins. He could make her want things with the slightest touch of his mouth, his wondrous mouth.

He *had* to care for her, at least just a little. A man couldn't kiss like this and not care, she told herself. She dug her fingers into his windbreaker, holding him close.

Telling himself not to, he allowed himself to touch her, to rub the tip of his thumb over the very softest part of her breast, which swelled out over her bra. He heard her sharp intake of breath and then the soft moan that followed. He filled his hand with her breast, desperately wanting her. If he could only let himself go completely, if he could just allow himself to forget. She reminded him of all the good things in life, of things that could be.

Of things that wouldn't be.

He forced himself to draw away just in the nick of time. Another second and there would be no turning back. He was behaving just like a reckless schoolboy, he thought deprecatingly. "Kate, I—"

She put her fingers on his lips. She ached, but it would pass, she told herself. Another time, when they were truly alone, she would press for a confrontation, but not now. "If you say you're sorry again, I'm afraid I'm going to have to take a strap to you, Mr. Marlowe."

He laughed aloud at the image that raised, and one of the boys moaned in his sleep.

"Shh," she hissed. "I don't know if I have another chorus left in me."

He drew her to the fire, and they sat down again. "No, I'm not sorry I kissed you."

"That's nice to know," she murmured. "I'm not sorry, either, as you might have already suspected." She rested her head against his shoulder again, content to stay like that until eternity ebbed away.

If he could only capture the peace that she brought him this moment and draw it out whenever he wavered, things would be all right. Or so he would have liked to believe. Believe. Before she had come, he had stopped believing in anything. And here she had him wanting to believe in happy endings again. "I've never met anyone like you before. You're open, you're warm, you're loving."

Kate stared drowsily into the fire. "You're not firing me, are you?"

"No, why would I be doing that?" He looked at her in astonishment.

She shrugged. "You've never said so many nice things to me at one time."

"If I haven't said them, then I've thought them."

Kate raised her head, wanting to see him, wanting to drink in everything about him. "I haven't mastered telepathy yet. It's nice to hear things." She noticed his expression soften. "What is it?"

"When I'm with you, I lose a little of myself."

"The cautious part?"

"Yes."

"Is that so bad?"

"Yes."

She ran her hand along his face gently. "No."

He wanted to shed the hold his fear had on him. He almost made it, and then something wouldn't let him. Something *always* held him back. "Oh, Kate, Kate, if only—"

"If only what?"

He turned away. "Nothing."

"Bryan, tell me." She paused, gathering courage. She put her hand on his arm, trying to maintain contact, any sort of contact. He *couldn't* close up on her again. He just couldn't. "Bryan, tell me about Jill."

He hadn't expected her to ask about that. "What?"

Kate never had trouble with honesty. She had bared her soul for him. "She's standing between us, and I want to know about her. I want to know what kind of a saint I have to measure up against." She took a breath to steady herself. Would he laugh at her? No, the Bryan who had just kissed her wouldn't laugh. "Because I mean to."

"Measure up?" He laughed in sad disbelief, shaking his head. "Oh, Kate. She wasn't like you. That is, she was, but she changed. Or maybe I just never let myself see what was really there. I was so in love with her that I'm not sure. God knows, I missed the signs."

"Signs?" Kate prodded, afraid that he would stop talking.

He stared into the flames. Yellow-and-red lights waved drunkenly in the air. "That she was unhappy. That what I wanted, what she *said* she wanted, she didn't. I was so sure of everything, of us. I had our whole lives mapped out.'' He shifted, looking at Kate urgently. ''It *was* what she wanted,'' he insisted, fighting a war within himself. ''At least, she told me she did. Maybe she really did,'' he added quietly.

Kate held his hand and kept her silence, urging him on with the look in her eyes, afraid to say anything that might resurrect the barriers again.

''I met her just shortly before I graduated from law school. We went together exactly two weeks before I asked her to marry me.'' He smiled at Kate ruefully. ''I've worked longer on briefs than I did on getting to know my future wife.''

''Some things are spontaneous.''

He laughed, self-deprecation evident in his face. ''Like combustion. That's what it was like. Like a fire, consuming, demanding.''

Kate felt envy for the woman who was now dead. Bryan had loved her in a way that was without reserve, in the way that *she* wanted him to love her.

''She got pregnant right away. I wanted a family. We both did. We had talked about it. We had *agreed*.'' He separated his hand from Kate's. She released it even though she didn't want to.

Bryan knotted his fingers together before him. ''But after Mike came along, Jill withdrew. She insisted on having a housekeeper. The housekeeper wound up taking care of the house and Mike. I thought maybe it was just some kind of postpartum depression, that it would pass. And for a while, it did. And then she became pregnant again.'' He took a deep breath, and Kate could feel his anguish, his confusion. ''Except this time, she didn't want to go through with it. I talked her into it. Begged her to keep the baby. She had the triplets because of me, because of what *I* wanted.''

He turned to look at Kate, wanting to make her understand. ''I wanted those boys, wanted a family. Jill began to feel trapped. She couldn't cope with the responsibilities that having young children put upon her. She wasn't an insensitive person, she just couldn't handle the situation she found herself in.''

He looked back into the fire, seeing the past rising up before him in the flames. Kate put her hand on his shoulder, and he became aware of her sitting there. He forced himself to go on.

''I didn't understand the depth of her feelings at the time, but I knew that something was wrong. I took her with me when I had to go to Hawaii to do some research for a case. I thought the break from the kids might do her some good. She finally broke down at dinner one night and told me exactly how she felt about everything. About feeling trapped and wanting to get away. I know now that it took a lot of courage on her part, but at the time, I didn't think of what she was going through, only how much she was hurting me.''

Kate's heart ached for the man who was struggling so hard to be fair to a memory.

''I told her to go,'' he echoed, his voice hollow. ''I was hoping that she'd argue with me, or that if she did leave for a while, she'd get it out of her system and come back to me. That she'd realize how much she loved and needed the boys and me. She left right away, to make arrangements for her future. I stayed to finish my work. In those days I let work come before family life. I paid for that." His voice dropped to barely a whisper. "The plane went down. There were no survivors."

She couldn't stand him blaming himself any longer. "Oh, Bryan, it wasn't your fault."

"But it *was*. If I hadn't forced her into my idea of a perfect life, if I had tried harder to help her, if I had made her stay, she might still be alive today."

"You thought you were doing what was best for both of you."

"But that doesn't change anything. It wasn't the best for both of us. Not for her."

"You had no way of knowing that," Kate insisted.

Let her go, Bryan, Kate begged silently. Leave some room for me. I take up such little space.

"I might be a crack lawyer, but I'm a poor judge of people, when it comes to my personal life."

"That's not true. One mistake—"

"Was one mistake too many," he retorted, his anguish finally pouring forth in full force. He had kept it locked up for so long.

"Bryan—" Where to begin? How to help him see that he wasn't at fault? Kate had never felt so helpless in her life.

Bryan rose and looked into the fire again. The embers were softening, about to die out. Like love, he thought, like promises made in the dark.

He squared his shoulders. "You'd better turn in. The boys'll want to get an early start back in the morning," he said without looking at her.

"I won't be dismissed, Bryan," she said firmly, trying to make him look at her. "The discussion isn't finished."

"I've nothing more to say," he said quietly before he walked away.

"Damn you," she murmured under her breath as she watched him. "Damn you and your male pride." She felt tears glistening in her eyes before she went into the tent.

Chapter Thirteen

He was avoiding her.

Since the evening of their talk by the campfire, Bryan had maintained a very clear, distinct separation between them. Whenever she had to discuss something about the boys or the household with him, he was friendly, but distant. She felt a sense of wariness coming from him. It was there in his eyes. It was almost as if he had managed to establish an invisible force field around himself. She could see him, but she couldn't touch him.

It was driving her crazy.

Bryan sat in his office, looking out the window. It was late. The day would be over soon. And so, he thought, would his relationship with Kate. He felt a sadness invading him and fought against it. He knew that he had opened himself up too far, had exposed the vulnerable layer that existed beneath the hard surface. He had told Kate things he had never said aloud even to himself. And in so doing, he had handed her a power over him, a power no one else had.

He didn't want her to have it.

And yet she did, by the very fact that he loved her. There was no use lying to himself about that. He knew the full extent of his feelings for her. But loving her brought with it apprehension, ghosts from the past and a host of "what ifs" to plague him. He lived with a fear of déjà vu. He had thought he knew Jill, yet he had been wrong, had read things into their relationship. By doing so, he had inadvertently forced things on her. He learned too late that she had been unhappy. And she had died. What if his judgment caused him to make the same mistake again? He couldn't risk it. More than anything, he couldn't risk *her*. He cared about Kate far too much.

It was best, he told himself, if he just let things go now.

He was driving her away and he knew it. He didn't want to, yet knew he had to.

Bryan hated the shackles that life had forged for him.

He sighed and tried to concentrate on the brief in front of him.

"What's on your mind, Katie?" Molly stopped what she was doing in the kitchen and studied Kate. "You seem preoccupied."

Kate took out a box of crackers from the pantry. She avoided her aunt's eyes. "Big exam tomorrow."

Molly cupped Kate's chin in her hand. "It's more than that. I've known you for twenty-six years. You've something on your mind. Out with it."

Kate sat down on the stool. There was an unfamiliar attitude of defeat in her manner. "I'm thinking of leaving."

"From here?" Molly asked in surprise.

"From here," Kate answered softly, her eyes downcast.

Molly wiped her hands on her apron and sat down next to Kate. "Why, in heaven's name?"

"Because I'm not doing any good."

"Ha, from what I hear from the other housekeepers, those boys were—"

"Just boys," Kate retorted defensively before realizing the sharpness of her tone. "Sorry, I tend to be overprotective where they're concerned, I guess."

"A mite, but also very, very good for them." The older woman drew her crescent brows together. "Why would you be thinking of leaving?"

Kate studied the cracker she was holding, turning it over and back again. Finally she said, "Because I'm not any good for him."

"Oh, it's the mister we're talking about now, is it?"

Kate's voice was dull. His rejection of her had hurt far more than she would have suspected. What's more, she felt she was hurting him by being there. She loved him too much to be the source of pain. "Yes."

"And what have you done that's so very, very bad for him?"

"I don't know, that's just it. I'm making him uncomfortable. I've done something, said something, that's made him back away. He treats me as if I'm some unwanted stranger."

Molly understood. "And it's breaking your heart."

Kate shrugged and looked out the window. Outside, the trees were bending in the wind. The hot winds from the desert were picking up. It was a Santa Ana condition. "I just don't want to be in a situation that's awkward."

"As I recall, that wouldn't be a first for you." Then Molly's tone softened. She reached over and squeezed Kate's hand. "Sleep on it, Kate. Don't do anything hasty."

Kate turned to look at her aunt. "Me? Never."

"And the Emerald Isle is made of green cheese."

"Maybe it is." Kate bit into the cracker.

"You're a blasphemous lass, you are."

"I had a scandalous aunt who taught me everything she knew."

For the moment, the two women laughed, pushing aside the seriousness of their subject. On her way out of the kitchen, Kate picked up a cookie, Trevor's favorite kind, off the carpet. One small bite had been taken out of it.

"Katie, he's gone!" Mike burst into Kate's room as she tried to steal a few hours to study.

Kate looked at Mike and saw that he was dragging an unwilling Trent in his wake. "Who's gone?"

"Trevor. He ran away."

She bolted to her feet, nearly overturning the chair at her desk. "Why?"

"Because he heard you and Molly talking," Mike said impatiently. "He told Trent that you were going away, just like Mom, so he was going away first."

"Oh God." She took hold of Trent's shoulders. Her grip was a little too hard. She saw him wince.

Kate lessened her hold. "Trent, why didn't you come to me right away?"

Trent's eyes began to fill with tears. "'Cause he made me promise not to tell."

"Hush, don't cry." She knelt down next to him. "Where did he go?"

Trent shook his head. "He wouldn't tell me."

No, she supposed he wouldn't. She struggled to organize her thoughts. For a moment, she considered calling Bryan, but what good would that do? He was probably still at the office and having him drive the thirty miles home wouldn't help find Trevor.

Where would a sad little boy go? Trevor had reverted to some of his old shyness when the household had become strained after the camping trip.

"The campgrounds!" Kate cried suddenly. "That's where we were all happy together." She felt sure that's where he was headed. But that was such a long way from there. Trevor would become hopelessly lost. With luck, he was somewhere in the area. If something hadn't happened to him. Kate felt her blood run cold.

She was already flying out of her room, her car keys in her hand.

"Hey, wait for me, Katie!" Mike cried, hurrying after her.

"Me, too!" Trent chimed in, running down the stairs behind them.

"And me!" From out of nowhere, Travis joined the group.

She wanted to tell them that they were all staying home, that they would only get in her way. But Trevor was their brother, and they were worried. She had no right to tell them not to come.

Molly saw the procession hurry by the kitchen on the way to the front door. "What's going on?" she called, crossing into the foyer.

"Trevor ran away from home," Travis announced importantly.

Molly clutched her clasped hands to her ample breasts. "Saints preserve us!"

"They'd better." Kate flung open the door. "If Bryan comes home, tell him the boys and I are out scouring the neighborhood."

She ran for the station wagon, the three boys directly behind her. They scrambled in as she got into the driver's side. For once, they weren't squabbling over who got the front seat.

"Now, how long ago did he leave?" she asked Trent.

"I can't tell time, Katie," the boy wailed.

She had forgotten. "Was the television on?"

"Yes."

Progress! "What were you watching?"

"Deputy Katt."

"That's on at five-thirty." She looked at her watch. "Half an hour." She bit her lip as she started the car. "Buckle up, boys, and keep your eyes peeled." She stepped on the gas.

"What does that mean?" Travis wanted to know.

"That means look for Trevor," Kate instructed.

She drove up the long road that she had once used to walk into the development. That seemed like a hundred years ago. Leaves and debris that had been whisked away from garbage cans unceremoniously denuded of their lids swirled around the streets in an ever-increasing tempo. The wind howled its growing temper tantrum. The Santa Anas, the devil winds they were called, were really coming on strong, Kate thought. It was something that occurred periodically in the area. Kate saw a branch on a eucalyptus tree break off and fly gracelessly to the ground across the street. She had to find Trevor before the winds became any stronger.

Where *was* he?

Guilt gnawed at her. Why hadn't she made sure no one was listening before she had poured out her thoughts to Molly? Trevor was so sensitive. Who knew what this would do to him? *If* she found him.

She *had* to find him.

At the outskirts of the development, Kate hesitated. There was a myriad of directions he could have gone off in. Which way should she take?

"What's the matter, Katie?" Travis asked uncertainly.

"Nothing. I'm just hoping my luck hasn't run out."

"What does luck have to do with it?" Trent wanted to know.

"A lot." Mumbling a prayer, she turned the station wagon north.

Within five minutes, she saw him, a lonely little figure trudging with his worn rabbit under his arm.

He had brought along his only friend, she thought, her heart breaking.

Kate pulled over to the curb and jumped out.

"Stay in here," she ordered, then ran after Trevor.

Catching up to him, she put her hands in her pockets and began to walk with him. She forced herself to take on a nonchalant air. "Kind of late to be going out for a walk, isn't it?"

"Not going for a walk," he muttered, grasping the

slipping rabbit tighter. He kept his eyes forward. "I'm going away."

"I'll miss you," she said simply.

"You won't be there."

The hurt accusation in his voice made her feel guiltier. "Yes, I will."

He stopped and looked at her. There was doubt mixed with confusion etched on his small features. "I thought you said you were leaving."

She dropped down to one knee. Kate put her hands on his arms and felt the boy stiffen. Like his father. It hurt. But there was a difference. She had had Trevor's trust and had thoughtlessly lost it again. "Well, I thought I was, but then I realized that I wouldn't be much good without my heart."

"Your heart?"

"Yeah. It's been kidnapped by four short guys named Marlowe." She smiled at him, praying she'd get a response. "Know them?"

A slow smile began to spread. "That's us."

"You betcha." She threw her arms around him then, letting all her fears out. "Oh Trevor, never, never do that to me again. I was so worried."

"Really?" Trevor sounded surprised and very, very pleased.

She blinked back tears as she looked at him, running her hand along his hair. "Really." She rose and put out her hand. "Now, what say we go back and tell Molly she doesn't have to call the police."

Trent put his hand in hers. "Would they have come with a siren and everything?"

"And everything." She began to lead him back to the car.

"Wow."

"But you would have missed it. You wouldn't
have been there," she reminded him.

"Oh."

She laughed. "Oh," she echoed. She gave up a
short prayer in thanksgiving. "Here's our lost lamb,"
she announced to the boys in the station wagon,
"home for supper." She seated herself behind the
wheel. "Now promise me no more excitement tonight. I've got a big exam to study for tomorrow. It's
a do-or-die final."

"What's a do-or-die final?"

"You'll find out in another ten years," she promised.

The boys were already in bed by the time Bryan
came home that night. Kate had made Molly promise
not to mention Trevor's disappearance. Telling him
would serve no purpose. He had enough on his mind
these days, it seemed. The matter was between Trevor
and her. Besides, she didn't feel like getting into any
discussion with Bryan tonight. She had to keep her
head straight for tomorrow's exam. She knew that
words with Bryan would only upset her, and then she
wouldn't be able to concentrate on her studies. This
final was very important to her.

It was the first night she hadn't come to talk to him
about the day's activities. His plan, he thought, was
working. He was succeeding in driving her away from
him emotionally.

So why wasn't he happy about it? he thought irritably.

He rose and turned off the light in the den. He
wasn't about to get anything accomplished tonight.

As he walked to his room, he stopped before her door. He could see light beneath the door. She was still up.

Bryan felt the urge to talk, the need to hear her voice, see her face. He raised his hand to knock and then let it drop.

It's for the best, he told himself as he walked away. For the best.

But he didn't believe it.

Kate fell asleep over her books and awoke with a terrible crick in her neck. She looked at the opened textbook that had served as her pillow. "Maybe the information seeped in through osmosis," she murmured, stretching. She gathered her notes together so that she might cram in one final review on the campus. Then she took a quick shower and got ready.

She glanced at her watch as she came down the stairs. Three hours away from zero hour.

She sailed into the kitchen. Though it was early, she saw that Bryan's coffee cup was there, half-empty. She exchanged looks with Molly.

"He left early."

"I see." Still playing games. Well, just maybe she'd have a talk with Mr. Bryan Marlowe after her exam was over and she had time to plan her approach. Things were going to have to change between them. She couldn't go on feeling like this.

"Molly, would you be a love and take the boys to school for me today? I really want some time to go over everything just once more."

Molly began setting the table for breakfast. "Don't give it another thought."

Kate grabbed a piece of toast from the pile on the serving plate and was about to dash out the front door.

That was when she heard the scream. Racing back the rest of the way, she collided with her aunt.

"It came from the backyard," the woman cried.

They hurried out the back door and found Trevor, Trent and Travis crowding around Mike, who sat on the ground, holding his left wrist with his right hand and fighting back tears.

"What happened?" Kate demanded.

"He jumped," Trent said.

"From the swing," Travis added.

Trevor pointed to Mike's wrist. "And landed on his hand."

"It made a funny noise, Katie," Mike cried.

"Here, let me see." Gently Kate took his left hand in both of hers. A bone was protruding in a place it had no business protruding from. She had seen it before when Patrick had tried his hand at acrobatics and failed. "Can you wiggle your fingers for me, Mike?"

The boy bit down on his lower lip. Slowly his fingers moved.

"That's very good, darling. Well, there's no school for you today." She looked up at her aunt, who was hovering next to her. "I think it's broken."

"Broken?" Mike's voice was high with fear.

She nodded. "You're going to have to go to the emergency room. The doctor will set it." She saw the fear in his eyes. "It's going to hurt, but it'll be better soon, I promise."

"Will you come with me, Katie?" he begged her.

She thought of her final. The professor had expressly stated that there would be no makeup exam. If she didn't take the final, she'd have to wait a whole year before the course was offered again. A whole year.

"I'll take the boy, Kate." Molly took charge. "You just go and take your exam."

"I don't wanna go without Katie." Mike finally broke down, not caring if his brothers saw him cry. It hurt and he was frightened.

"Honey, Molly can—"

Kate stopped. Sure Molly was capable of taking him and holding his hand. But he wanted her. How could she desert him now when he needed her most? Did a piece of paper mean that much to her? Where was her compassion, where were all the things she wanted to bring to this shining profession she aspired to? Kate made up her mind.

"Molly can take your brothers to school. You and I are going to the hospital."

"Katie—" Molly protested.

"I don't have time to argue, Aunt Molly, he's in pain." Gently she helped Mike to his feet. "Help me get him to the car." She put one arm around the boy's shoulders. "It's going to be all right, Mike." She kissed the top of his head reassuringly. "And you'll get a neat cast for all your friends to sign—the ones who can, of course."

"He's *where*?" Bryan had to restrain himself from shouting into the telephone.

"Kate took Mike to the emergency room at St. Sebastian's Hospital," Molly repeated. "We think he's broken his wrist."

Bryan was already on his feet, ready to hang up the phone. "I'm on my way—"

"There's something else that you should know, Mr. Marlowe."

"Oh God, there's more?"

"A lot more. She's taking him there even though I could have."

He didn't understand what Molly was driving at. "And?"

"She had a final today, but Mike wanted her with him. She wouldn't be talked out of going. And last night, Trevor ran away."

"*What?* Why didn't anyone tell me?" he demanded angrily.

"She didn't want to upset you. Said you had enough on your mind. Trevor ran away because he thought Kate was leaving."

First Mike, then Trevor, now Kate. Had the world gone crazy in the last twenty-four hours? "Why would she want to leave?" But even as he asked the question, he knew.

"That's something I think you're going to have to discuss with her."

He could hear the barely suppressed accusation in the older woman's voice. "I fully intend to. Anything else?"

"Yes. I'd wake up and smell the coffee if I were you, Mr. Marlowe."

The line went dead. The old woman was as crazy as her niece, he thought irritably. Bryan paused long enough to tell his secretary his destination, then hurried to the parking lot.

Leaving. Molly's words came echoing back to him. Kate was thinking of leaving. The thought of life without her went through him like a sharp knife.

Got what you wanted, didn't you?

No, now it wasn't what he wanted. And Kate wasn't the crazy one. He was if he let her go. He had been turning his back on someone wonderful because he had turned into a virtual emotional coward. He had had the real thing in the palm of his hand, and now she was thinking of leaving.

Well, she wasn't, by God, not if he had to chain her to the house and plead with her to reconsider.

Kate was just writing out a check at the cashiers' window when Bryan hurried into the emergency reception area.

He caught hold of Kate by the arm. "How is he?"

She tried hard not to react to the fact that he was touching her. Contact with him, she discovered, hurt. "Mending now, thank heavens."

"Where is he?" She pointed into the waiting area. "Wait right here," Bryan instructed.

She saluted. "I'm not going anywhere."

"No," he said firmly, "you're not."

His words brought an anticipatory shiver down her spine, but she told herself that she was reading things into his meaning. That had been her problem all along. A person could dream only so long before she finally woke up. And she had. She had had a lot of time to think this morning. Daylight was streaming into the window of her life. She was the governess, and that was that. She was just going to have to come to terms with that fact if she was going to stay on.

She watched as father and son exchanged an embrace and words. And then Bryan came back to her. Odd that Mike didn't follow, she thought.

"He says he's all right."

"He's a brave boy."

"Molly told me that you skipped taking your exam to bring Mike here."

Kate shrugged casually. She didn't want his grati-
tude if it came out of pity. "I hate taking exams."

"Don't make light of it. I know what that degree
means to you." He hesitated. "Thank you."

"There's nothing to thank me for," she said a bit
too tartly. "I love Mike. I love all the boys. To be
loved and needed by someone is far more important
to me than a final grade or ultimately a piece of paper
giving me a title. I wouldn't be much of a child psychologist if I ignored the pleas of a child, now would
I?"

But he knew it was more than that. It had been all
along. "Why didn't you tell me that Trevor ran
away?"

All the anger, all the hurt, came to the surface. "I
haven't been able to tell you much of anything all
week. You've been burying yourself in your work,
away from me. What's worse, away from the boys."

Fear of losing her made him lose his temper. "This
wasn't just some trivial report on a successful trip to
the mall." He saw her eyes flare and realized his mistake. He hadn't meant to say it that way. "I'm sorry.
They're not trivial reports. Everything you've done
so far has been very, very important."

She softened in the face of his words. "You're taking the fun out of this argument."

"I don't want to argue. I want to apologize. God,
what an idiot I've been."

"Is that in the general sense, or are you alluding
to a particular moment?"

She was getting back at him. "I deserve that."
Here was a lady who wasn't about to change her position on things. She wasn't going to change before

his eyes once he married her. She would always be Kate, and that was what he loved about her.

"That and more."

"Agreed." He took her face between his hands and looked at her as if seeing her for the first time.

Although she cherished his nearness, she was afraid of misconstruing things again. "People are beginning to stare, Mr. Marlowe."

"Let them." He didn't care about appearances. All he cared about was getting Kate to stay. Permanently. "How would you feel about getting a piece of paper giving you another sort of title?"

"Such as?" she asked cautiously.

He released her. "I guess in my clumsy way, I'm asking you to take on the title of Mrs. Marlowe." He saw her eyes open wide in surprise. "Kate, I'm asking you to marry me." He saw no answer in her eyes, only astonishment. Had he lost her before he had time to appreciate her? In desperation, he drew on the only weapon he knew he had. "The boys need you."

She stiffened. Was that it? "The boys have me, and that isn't a good enough reason to get married." Kate pulled away, anger highlighting her eyes. "Don't worry, Mr. Marlowe, I won't be asking for a raise, and I'll be needing this job even longer than I anticipated I would." Kate turned and walked toward Mike, her gait brisk, her indignation evident in the way she held herself.

"Would it change matters any if I told you that I need you?" Bryan called out after her.

Kate stopped walking. She let the smile in her heart rise up to her lips and spread across her face.

Bryan came up to her, ignoring the stares of various people in the room. The only thing that mattered was that Kate understood what she meant to him. "Need you and want you and love you. Damn it, Kate, I've been afraid to love you, afraid that I'd ruin your life if I did."

"You big idiot, don't you know that you'd only ruin it if you didn't love me?"

"Is that a yes?"

She let her voice drop low. "If you're this slow at your cases, Mr. Marlowe, I'm surprised that you win any of them at all." She put her arms around his neck and raised herself up on her toes, her mouth a scarce breath away from his. "That is most definitely a yes."

She heard Mike cheering in the background as Bryan kissed her in the middle of the emergency room.

* * * * *

SPECIAL EDITION

Stories of love and life, these powerful novels are tales that you can identify with—romances with "something special" added in!

Fall in love with the stories of authors such as **Nora Roberts, Diana Palmer, Ginna Gray** and many more of your special favorites—as well as wonderful new voices!

Special Edition brings you entertainment for the heart!

SSE-GEN

SILHOUETTE® Desire®

Do you want...

Dangerously handsome heroes

Evocative, everlasting love stories

Sizzling and tantalizing sensuality

Incredibly sexy miniseries like **MAN OF THE MONTH**

Red-hot romance

Enticing entertainment that can't be beat!

You'll find all of this, and much *more* each and every month in **SILHOUETTE DESIRE**. Don't miss these unforgettable love stories by some of romance's hottest authors. Silhouette Desire—where your fantasies will always come true....

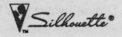

▼ *Silhouette* ROMANCE™

What's a single dad to do when he needs a wife by next Thursday?

Who's a confirmed bachelor to call when he finds a baby on his doorstep?

How does a plain Jane in love with her gorgeous boss get him to notice her?

From classic love stories to romantic comedies to emotional heart tuggers, **Silhouette Romance** offers six irresistible novels every month by some of your favorite authors! Such as…beloved bestsellers **Diana Palmer, Annette Broadrick, Suzanne Carey, Elizabeth August** and **Marie Ferrarella,** to name just a few—and some sure to become favorites!

Fabulous Fathers…Bundles of Joy…Miniseries… Months of blushing brides and convenient weddings… Holiday celebrations… You'll find all this and much more in **Silhouette Romance**—always emotional, always enjoyable, always about love!

SR-GEN